D0990675

CHRISTINE CRAIG is Jamaican, an honours graduate of the University of the West Indies, where she majored in English and Mass Communications. Her first published work was children's fiction, *Emmanuel and His Parrot*, which came out in 1970. She has since had two more works of children's fiction published as well as having researched, written and presented a regular series of Jamaican history stories for children on television. She has had a keen interest in feminist and health topics which led to several non-fiction publications and training manuals. She is also the author of numerous short stories and poems written for adults which have appeared in Jamaican, British and American anthologies and journals. Her first collection of poetry, *Quadrille for Tigers*, came out in 1984 in the States. In 1989, she was awarded a fellowship to the International Writers Programme at the University of Iowa, USA. She now lives in Florida. *Mint Tea* is her first collection of short stories.

CHRISTINE CRAIG

MINT TEA

And Other Stories

HEINEMANN

Heinemann International Literature and Textbooks
A Division of Heinemann Educational Books Ltd
Halley Court, Jordan Hill, Oxford OX2 8EJ

Heinemann: A Division of Reed Publishing (USA) Inc.
361 Hanover Street, Portsmouth, NH 03801–3912, USA

Heinemann Educational Books (Nigeria) Ltd
PMB 5205, Ibadan
Heinemann Educational Boleswa
PO Box 10103, Village Post Office, Gaborone, Botswana

LONDON   EDINBURGH   PARIS   MADRID
ATHENS   BOLOGNA   MELBOURNE   SYDNEY
AUCKLAND   SINGAPORE   TOKYO

First published by Heinemann International Literature and Textbooks
in 1993

Series Editor: Adewale Maja-Pearce

British Library Cataloguing in Publication Data
A catalogue record for this book is available from the British Library.

AFRICAN WRITERS SERIES and CARIBBEAN WRITERS SERIES and their
accompanying logos are trademarks in the United States of America of
Heinemann: A Division of Reed Publishing (USA) Inc.

ISBN 0435 989 324

Cover design by Touchpaper
Cover illustration by Chloë Cheese
Author photograph by Bea Lim

Phototypeset by Cambridge Composing (UK) Ltd, Cambridge
Printed and bound in Great Britain
by Cox & Wyman Ltd, Reading, Berkshire

93 94 10 9 8 7 6 5 4 3 2 1

CONTENTS

~ for Rachael and Rebecca

Where can we meet my brother,
my lover, my friend
to make something new together.

I will meet you on the road
for I have done with waiting.
I will help you with your load
and welcome your greeting.
I will meet you on the road
for I have shaped my journey.

Sister Mary

Sunday morning and the heat had not come up fully in the hills. Sister Mary walked resolutely but without haste. Her strong legs had grown from the spindly little girl legs of some forty-five years past. They had walked the same route as they shaped into the legs of a young woman. The feel of the road was in her bones, days carrying the basket to the main road to meet the truck going to Papine market. Evenings walking to the cross roads to meet Linton coming up from his ground. She was eighteen, he was twenty and although they did not say much to each other, it became known that they were 'talking'.

They lived well together and in the early days they had turned readily towards each other in the double bed. But as the years passed and still no baby could start between them, she began to turn away from him. Linton was a quiet, easy-going man. He grew good crops on his small piece of land and dreamed of getting a bigger piece of land where he could go into livestock. On Saturdays when he had had a few drinks in the one shop that became a bar on Saturday evenings, he would grow optimistic and expansive. Somehow that week he was going to put away some money. In no time at all he would have a little savings and he would go to the Agricultural Office. He heard there was land to lease and he would apply for some.

On Sunday, as Linton read the *Sunday Gleaner* carefully and listened to the radio, he would loose heart. Everything was getting so political and violent. He heard that town youths were being given good agricultural land and plenty ginnalship was going on. The established farmers complained that the youth were bringing pure trouble out to the country parts. Thieving and bad living and growing so much ganja. Next thing the police were out there and the regular farmers, who used to grow their little bit of herbs, began to feel threatened. Linton, like Mary, had grown up in Comfort Hill. He knew the district like the back of his hand. He knew the people and they knew him. Even for more land, he didn't know if he should move. Her trips down to Papine confirmed the news Linton relayed to her from the *Gleaner*. Things were bad. Pure cuss cuss was going on in the market and prices were rising faster than bread in the oven.

They lived well together and for the first few years Linton didn't think about not having children. There was time, plenty of time. As the eldest, he had had to leave school at fifteen when his mother died, and it seemed to him at the time that he would never be finished looking after his four younger brothers and sisters. Cissie, the sister that followed him, didn't get much schooling, but between them they managed to put food on the table and they managed, somehow, to stay together even when there was no money for school books, clothes, or shoes.

Linton remembered one evening when Cissie, for no good reason as far as he could see, burst out in a terrible temper with Leroy, the twelve year old. She beat him mercilessly and then she threw herself on the floor and raged and wept. She said, God help her, she would never have children, it was pure work and crosses and maybe Mama wouldn't have died if she hadn't had so many children. Well, that was all in the past now. Cissie went to Canada on the domestic scheme and Linton didn't hear from her much. She had not stayed long in domestic work and, last thing he heard, she was managing a small restaurant and doing very well. But there was a deep bitterness in Cissie and Linton felt she wanted to forget about Comfort Hill that had been no comfort to a fifteen year old with three young brothers and sisters to bring up.

So at first, Linton had not thought about it much. But gradually he began to be worried about it. He would pick a quarrel with Mary, about something trivial, and sooner or later he would get to the real point. He would tell her that he was going to find another woman who wasn't barren. His younger brother had four children and he couldn't get one of his own yet. Sometimes she said nothing and wept. Sometimes she would be angry.

'Go on den nuh. Is who stoppin you. You see me have any old rope to tie you down wid? Go on man. Go find a young gal. Is dat you well want anyway.'

Linton would turn away as if he wasn't talking to her.

'I see a chile yesterday. Just yesterday, an she well ripe an pretty. An so I notice her she notice me too . . .'

The anger between them would loom up and fill the small house until Mary thought her heart would burst.

Once, after a particularly bitter quarrel, Mary dressed carefully and walked out. She got a lift in a truck to Papine, walked through the gates of the big hospital and eventually found the Family Planning Clinic. She was thirty and childless. She sat in a crowded room with girls of twenty who had three children already, women of thirty who had six and Mary listened to them talking about how they couldn't afford to have any more. She felt as if a place inside of her was weeping and weeping and she could not speak. When it was her turn, she went into a little cubicle and spoke to the nurse. The nurse kept asking questions and filling up a form and then she told her to wait and see the doctor. Mary waited. It was afternoon, she was hungry, tired. She watched other women leaving and still she sat there.

Her name was called and again she went into a cubicle. The doctor was very young. He asked her some questions and his voice was so unexpectedly kind that suddenly the whole day of waiting, the years of empty waiting, poured out of her eyes. The doctor said, 'Don't upset yourself, it's all right. Let me have a look and we'll see what can be done.'

It was so many years later but walking down the road she remembered it so clearly. Her embarrassment that this young doctor was looking into her naked body, her fear that he would find something terrible there inside of her. But when she was dressed he only said, 'Everything seems fine. Yes, just fine. Would your husband come and have some tests done?'

Going home that evening Mary almost laughed out loud at herself. How come she had never thought perhaps it was Linton who couldn't make the baby start. She knew, and didn't want to know that he had been with other women, but she knew that none of them had made a baby for him. After that her feelings for Linton changed. A softness grew inside of her, a kind of compassion for her big, strong man. Mary was thirty, her body was short and firm, her movements strong and capable. Her skin was smooth and black and when she smiled her cheeks made two smooth, rounded mounds as if she was sucking two plum seeds at the same time. All Mary ever told Linton about the trip to the hospital was that the doctor had said she was fine.

'Must be just God's will,' she said.

After that trip to the doctor she turned towards Linton with a new warmth. She would stroke his back and tease him gently until he was seized with passion for this woman he had known for so long yet was suddenly a laughing, teasing stranger. He began to wonder if she had taken another man and the idea grew like a nagging pain at the back of his mind. One day he came in, washed himself and sat exhausted on the porch. No rain for months and the ground was so hard to dig. Still he had got it planted and now the seedlings were getting straggly because they should have been planted out at least two weeks ago. Mary brought him out a big tumbler of lemonade; he took it and drank it without a word. She suddenly put her hand on his cheek, 'No mind me love, it soon goin rain.' Linton looked at her, her eyes were shiny and her mouth slightly parted with little beads of sweat on the top lip.

'Mary you have a man?' The words came out all choked and mixed up.

She took her hand away abruptly and said, 'No, you's the only man I ever have an I happy wid you. Why I should suddenly turn bad woman?'

4

They didn't speak about it any more and two nights later Linton woke up and heard the rain falling, softly at first and then it seemed to increase with a steady drumming power. Linton lay and heard the rain falling and he was moved with a great feeling as if he himself was the land and the rain was falling on him, washing away years of hardship and endless struggle to just get through each year, to grow enough to live on. He could hear Mary's breath soft on the pillow beside him, and, as he listened to her breathing and the rain falling, he felt strong and happy and in a curious way, free as he had never been before.

Things went well for them that year. They built a little shop and stocked it with food, some basic hardware items and Mary insisted on fixing up a shelf with aspirin, bay rum, Vicks and a few other household medicines. Nobody had much money at Comfort Hill and the shop took a while to start making money. Even then, they just about had enough for buying new stock. Mary managed the shop and Linton did the accounts once a week. In time, he started saving a little in the Credit Union which was in the nearest big town.

They had always been fairly regular church goers but Mary began to go every Sunday and she began to read her Bible with a special sort of zeal. Linton watched with a faint distrust. For the last few years, she had been such a strong, loving woman, he hoped she wasn't going to get all sanctimonious and you couldn't do this and you couldn't do that because it wasn't Christian.

The troubles of the city began to be felt as far up as Comfort Hill. It was hard to put an exact date on it, or even to name what the trouble was. It was a sort of general anxiety. Tales of violence were reported in the crisp radio announcer's voice which made them seem somehow official but somehow unreal. These things must be happening if they were on the radio and in the *Gleaner*. The *Gleaner* said it was all socialist wickedness, that the country was headed for communism, like Cuba. Mary said

5

communism was Godlessness and if that happened no one would be able to go to church again and they would all be in the devil's domain.

People talked politics, but without too much conviction, for whichever party was in, nothing new happened in Comfort Hill. The children still had to walk miles to a crowded one-roomed school. True electricity had come but along with it came bills that demanded payment and a person had to walk miles into town to pay it. There was talk of land being distributed, but it must be happening someplace else. In the shop people talked more and bought less.

'Miss Mary, you hear how de politicians a give de likkle young boy dem guns? Yes, is so I hear, and nobody can sleep a nighttime in dem beds.'

'Is true yes, but is both sides mix up ina de wickedness. I hear say no matter if you live in a fancy house or if you live down in a tenement yard, you not safe a nighttime.'

'What you talking bout nighttime. My cousin and de whole family, dem house get rob ina de broad daylight. Me say, Maisie at work an de littlest one, dem call him Bigeye, him come running clear to where she working to tell her say de yout dem bruk ina de house an mash up everything an rough up de poor likkle pickney till dem nearly dead wid fright. Now anybody every hear my crosses. Maisie don' have one ting in dis world cept plenty pickney. Who woulda go dere fe tief? Tief what!'

'Den why she doan move outa town? Dat city is pure badness dese days.'

'An where she fe go? What work she a go get ina country? Her tiefin father, I know is me uncle, but God's truth, him done sell out de likkle land shoulda been for Maisie and dem. Nobody know which part him gone wid de money, but dem have neither land nor money, so what you can do ina case like that?'

Everyone agreed that Maisie was in a really bad way and the conversation, having moved from the general to the particular plight of Maisie moved on to embrace all women who had to survive in the city.

'De Lord knows why Jamaica woman have it so hard. No matter what she do, is she one leave wid de pickney. De man dem all bout de place an doan business bout pickney 'till dem come through all right. Den when is gradiation time, see dem turn up bright an bold – "see me son deh . . ."'

'Well what I say is, some a dem woman bring it on demselves. Dem too like walk street ina all kind a tight frock. An dem doan business how de man stay as long as dem tink him have few dollars ina him pocket.'

'Me dear, you have fe watch you likkle gal pickney dese days. Dem ready to feel seh dem is big somebody an dress off like city woman. I tell you, right here ina dis likkle districk, dem have some big man, what shoulda know better, ready to swoop down like John Crow on de likkle young gal dem.'

Mary did more listening than talking, but when the conversation got on home ground and was headed straight for name calling gossip, she usually tried to change the subject.

Linton was seldom in these conversations as he had found a new interest in his life. From keeping the shop accounts and making regular visits to the Credit Union, he became known as having 'a good head for figures,' and what is more, he could 'write a good hand'. Some of the other farmers began discussing business with him and he became something of an unofficial accountant in the district. Mary was proud of this development and would make quite a big thing of delivering any messages that came for him at the shop.

'Mr Boyd send word to say that he asking you to stop by him house in de week.'

If Linton was not forthcoming with any information, she would probe gently.

'Don't him is de one tek over Boysie Jones' farm way over Topside? But dat is a big place you know Linton. Wonder what him want to see you about.'

Linton was non-communicative. He could only 'indicate' that there were 'private business matters' to be discussed and he could not 'divulge' what was told to him in the 'strikest confidence'. This secretiveness pleased Mary as it convinced her that

7

Linton was held in high esteem and it was quite right that he shouldn't talk people's business.

Mary was now forty-five. She was Sister Mary who ran the shop and still went to market on Fridays. She was happy and yet she began to feel restless. She was happy that Linton felt fulfilled but she wanted something more and she felt guilty about it. She didn't know what it was, but sometimes when Linton was sleeping, she would get up, pull an old frock over her nightdress, and sit on the porch. Looking out over the dark hills or up into the endless stars she tried to think what it was. The tales from the city were getting worse. Some Kingston youths turned up in the next district and captured some land. It was said that they were gunmen hiding out and people began to be more careful about locking up things, including their children. Mary went to church and listened to Rev. Samuels preach and although he said the Lord was a terrible and vengeful god, she felt that the Lord wouldn't let them perish. So what was it then, she wondered. She looked up at the stars and they were silent. For so many years she had longed for a sign, that she would get pregnant and start a family. The bible had stories like that and she prayed for a miracle. Now at forty-five she had given up that dream and the space it left in its going was filled with irritability and sadness.

Sister Mary walked resolutely but without haste to church. It had been dry for months but a little rain had fallen over the last few days. It was enough to make the place look green and Mary felt suddenly young and light hearted. The dark thoughts that troubled her seemed to lift in the daylight and the whole world looked young and bright.

'Sister Mary, excuse me mam but Reverend Samuels . . .' Sister Gertie's son Donald was rushing down the road towards her. He was polished up for church and looking very important.

'The Reverend says he been call away to Topside an Brother Thomas tek down sick, so could you please tek de service dis morning mam. Him say.'

Donald came to an abrupt end and Sister Mary thanked him for the message. Having delivered the message, Donald was unsure what to do next and trailed along behind her. Sister Mary sent him on ahead to tell the church elders and tried to compose her thoughts. She didn't have any sermon prepared, why had he asked her, and it was only her regular old navy dress she had on, but what would people say. Well, there didn't seem to be any choice after all, it was the Lord's work.

The church was a small, solid, square concrete building with large windows already thrown open for the service. Set up on a little hill, Mary approached it slowly. Donald had done his job and the people assembled already knew. They greeted her warmly and if anyone was feeling a bit resentful about Reverend Samuel's choice, it didn't show. Mary looked out at the graves sloping down the hillside and her glance caught a nightingale. It landed on her mother's grave and started its full-chested song. The buoyancy of the early morning swept through her again to be replaced immediately with nervousness.

Sister Mary conducted the service. The church was almost full and everyone knew the responses and the hymns. Then the church fell silent as Sister Mary came forward to give the sermon.

'Brothers and sisters,' she said. 'We give thanks today that the Lord has blessed us with rain. The green leaves are coming up in the fields and the flowers are showing their pretty faces for the Lord. And I say, "Let us sing unto the Lord a new song." Like the birds of the air that make music for the Lord, we must sing a new song. Wickedness surrounds us, but still we have much to be thankful for. Let us turn away from sorrow and despair and praise the Lord.'

'Praise the Lord,' said a deep voice.

'Praise His holy name,' said another.

Sister Mary spoke of joy and thanksgiving. She mentioned by name those who were sick or troubled and asked for prayers for them. She did not speak of sin and hellfire and as the congregation listened a feeling of joy and hopefulness spread through the church. She had to pause often as the feeling broke out.

'Praise the Lord.'

9

'Thank you Jesus.'

Sister Mary brought the service to an end and the congregation streamed out into the hot midday sun. Her friends came to shake her hand and congratulate her and they walked home slowly together. Her heart was soaring and she felt a sort of completeness inside her. As she walked she prayed that it wasn't false pride to be so happy. She told Linton about it almost offhandedly but he heard about it for days out on the road. People said they had gone to church as poor sinners but when Sister Mary spoke it was as if each person was the happiest and most blessed person in the world. It was a natural gift, they said. Sister Mary had the power. The power of the Word.

Case Study

Ellie Simpson, age twenty-two. Living in poverty, but not despair. One night of love with a soldier. When she told him she was pregnant, he ran her.

'G'way. How I fe know is mine? How much more men you sleep wid since me? You never hear about abortion? Get one.'

Ellie Simpson, age twenty-five. One daughter Marva, age two years.

'Me seh, de chile pretty, she pretty can' done. She don' have a ting fe she modda. Well you know Ellie not a bad looking chile, don' mind dat she black like me. But dis baby Marva is one pretty little brown skin baby. Yes man. Me sey she brown like when you mix chocolate tea an you have plenty milk fe mix it wid. Den so de skin brown, so de hair brown too and sof an curly. No missis, anyway you see dat baby you would must want tief her.'

Ellie left school in fourth form. Her mother was sick, sick and tired. Ellie heard about a job at the Hotel Nova. Chambermaid at $45 per week so Mama could take a break. And any road, the little exams don't mean anything. Plenty girls leave school all three years ago with all five subjects on the certificate an they still can' get no job. This job just fall braps into her lap and she would be too fool not to take it. Look how long Mama one doing everything for me. She well need a ease.

11

'Ellie, you mad or what? I soon get better an can go back to work. (Domestic, nice family, low pay). How much time I fe tell you education is de only ting can save poor people. You tink I have it hard for so long so you can go leave school wid you long, empty hand dem?'

But Ellie is taking the bus every day, like all the other working women. Shoes neat, new dress, hair just done. (Me will give you $10 now and de rest next week. OK? Tanks me darling. You know is work I'm going?) Neat uniform hanging up at work and everywhere so clean. Curtains and carpets and pictures on the wall. Ellie's favourite room had deep pink spreads on the bed and a picture of a little brown-skinned girl. She was holding a red hibiscus flower in her hand and her smile was so pretty Ellie would stop dusting and smile back. She would imagine herself getting married, Del would do her hair and Miss Dawkins would make her a lovely long dress with a veil. And they would go to live in a house with a bedroom just like this one and a bathroom with soft, clean towels. And they would have a little girl . . .

'Ellie, how many times have I told you to fold the spread under the pillow first. Lord give me strength. I talk till I tired but these girls nowadays . . . they have everything too easy, that's the whole trouble.'

Ellie fixed the spread quickly, dropped her eyes.

'Sorry Mistress Bowen.'

Mrs Bowen made a quick inspection and swept out. Not a bad girl that one. At least she had some manners and some schooling.

At lunch time Ellie ate with the other girls at a special table fixed up at the side of the kitchen. The food was so good she wished she could take some home. But Mr Barrett the chef had an eye like a looking-glass. Once he saw Millie slipping some chicken into her pocket and he stood there and quarrelled with her right in front of everybody. Ellie felt it for her. The poor girl was so ashamed you could see she was trying hard not to cry.

Some of the waiters would try to get fresh sometimes, but Ellie wasn't interested. She was waiting to 'fall in love'. She didn't see much of the guests. They were mostly businessmen, staying at the hotel for a few days only. Ellie got to understand that one of the senior waiters had a deal going where he would line up a girl for a guest, and get a percentage. Ellie avoided him, she dreaded him asking her. Now and again a family would stay over. A Venezuelan family came for a week. They had heavy accents and two beautiful children. Two little boys with big dark eyes and straight dark hair. Ellie would take them out in the afternoon so the parents could have a nap. Eduardo and Roberto. Once Ellie went over in the evening to baby-sit. She made up a game for them to play. They would open a magazine, she would point to something on the page and whoever said the word first would get a point. 'Girl', 'muchacha'. They shouted and laughed and Ellie had to pretend to get cross to get them to settle down and go to sleep. She watched television while they slept and would look over at them and feel very happy. But she wasn't sure why. When the family was ready to leave she felt sad. Eduardo and Roberto. They shook hands politely and then they threw their arms around her and hugged and kissed her.

'What a way you wrap up ina dat family Ellie. Why you don' ask dem if dem want you to go work wid dem.'

'In Venezuela Mama! Dem not goin' want dat.'

So she didn't ask and later she was sorry and thought about them. Living in a big modern city and talking Spanish all the time.

Ellie had been working at Hotel Nova for about a year when Mama got a new 'friend'. Everyone called him Mr T and while he seemed alright, Ellie never really took to him. Mr T didn't bring much of anything into the house but Mama was working and she was happy.

Ellie put some money into partner* and when her turn came she bought some plates and curtains for the front room. Sometimes Ellie and her friends went to the movies but mostly it was work and home. Then things started to get difficult. Fewer and fewer guests were coming to the hotel. Mr T said, 'is politicks. Damn politicks mashing up de country. So much violence and

* Traditional, informal saving scheme among women friends.

13

shortage everywhere. No wonder de foreigners dem don' come any more.'

Ellie was laid off at the hotel. Mrs Bowen said she was sorry and anyway that things got better she would send and let her know. Ellie drifted. No job. Mr T going on like he owned the place and only Mama bringing in a little money.

The next year Ellie got a few months' work back at the hotel and she started going out with Sammy. He was a waiter at the hotel, good looking and ambitious. One day Ellie went to tidy up a room and found that the guest was still there.

'Sorry to disturb you sir, I'll come back later.'

'No, no, you didn't disturb me. Come here a minute honey.'

She went inside. A fat man with grey hair was laying in bed. He wanted Ellie to do it and he would give her $20 American. Ellie was so shocked she just stood and looked at him. He offered more and Ellie ran. 'But what a feisty old man. Lord God, him must be mad. What I woulda want wid him!'

Ellie kept thinking about it and eventually she told Sammy.

'Eh, how you so fool! You don' even know if you working next month, you shoulda tek de money yes.'

Ellie broke up with Sammy and she was once more out of a job. Something hardened in her and whenever she ran into her hotel friends she would try to give the impression of being very wise and experienced, and yes she was just fine. In the evenings she would sit around with the older women in the yard and listen as they talked about how times were hard. But more people were home in the days and quarrels broke out all the time. It was pure green banana and mackerel time and sometimes there wasn't even dry crackers in the house to eat.

No work. What certificates do you have? Can you type? No work. And the men and women in jobs looked at her with hard, critical eyes. The looks said they knew she had little in her home to eat. They knew she was wearing her only decent dress and that she had to hide her left foot behind the right one when she sat down because the heel was so worn down. No job, hard and

14

critical like even looking was somehow an affront to the people safe in jobs.

It was late afternoon and Ellie started walking home. A car pulled up and offered her a lift. Tall, handsome, brown-skinned man. A soldier. Why didn't they stop and have a drink and avoid the traffic. She knew what he wanted and she didn't care. She was too tired and in the whole empty world here was a man smiling and speaking gently to her.

Marva is two years old. Mr T has left and once more it's Mama and Ellie. In the evenings Ellie sits on the front step, rubbing a piece of mint between her fingers. The whole yard is women and children trying to live. The men pass through briefly, strutting and showing off 'till the big belly is on you then they disappear.

The women pretend not to care. Sometimes a woman would say to Ellie, 'Dat baby of yours need a little flesh on her body. Come give her dis little piece of chicken.' At first, Ellie resented it, but then she realized it was kindness. They didn't want to seem soft, to seem that they were making a favourite of the latest addition, but Mama and Ellie enjoyed a new kind of friendship with the other women in the yard. No one wanted their daughter to bring home a fatherless baby. But once it happened a space was made and life continued.

Ellie takes Marva to the Independence celebration at the stadium. Ellie is excited by the singing and dancing, hundreds of schoolchildren sing 'Jamaica Land We Love' and her eyes grow misty. Two rows up above her in the stands the soldier stands with his nice, up-town wife. Their son is in the scouts display, drilling and marching like a miniature soldier. The soldier sees them and as he sees Marva he recognizes himself with a strange stirring. A one-time fling and there is a baby girl looking just like him.

Raymond tries to forget about them, but a few weeks later he is at Ellie's yard. At first she is very hostile. He thought she was an easy girl, wanted her to have an abortion. Now he sees how pretty the baby is he wants to play Daddy. Mama urges her to be more forgiving. After all, what harm could it do for him to see her sometimes.

For the first time in his life Raymond was in love. He couldn't stop thinking about his baby. Look at how she had taken to him right from the start! Those round, brown eyes and her little arm around his neck! Raymond thought about her endlessly.

For the first time he started thinking about all those stories of men who neglect their own children. 'Damn disgrace.' He knew he must do the right thing for his daughter. His wife Coleen was a good, educated, middle-class woman and they both knew why the marriage had worked so well. He liked her class, her good job, her knowledge of how to run a good home. She knew her school friends had at first snickered over his dropped 'h's', but they envied her this big, handsome, macho man. Raymond was careful how he broke the news to her. After the grieving and the anger, Coleen began to see his point of view. He had made a mistake and should now do the right thing. They could give her a good home, send her to a good school, rescue her from yard life. Their only child was seven and it didn't look as if they were going to have any more children. They imagined how pleasant their home would be with a pretty little baby in it. Their friends might be a little scandalized but since they were doing the right thing, what did it matter what they thought.

Raymond was genuinely amazed at Ellie's reaction.

'Give her to you! Man you mad. She not a ting you know. If she had been black and look like me you wouldn' even notice her. But you see yourself in her an you want her.'

After he left, Ellie and Mama raged. They raged against the man but inwardly they raged against their poverty. That's what he was going to use to take Marva away from them. He could put her in a pretty, up-town house and send her to a private prep school. She would grow up as a pretty, brown-skinned girl with a fancy home to take friends to, a TV and two bathrooms stacked with soft towels and nice smelling soap.

Ellie took a shower in the one shower shared by five families. Outside the shower, in a kind of alcove, a piece of string stretched between two nails served as a place to hang your clean clothes when you bathed. Ellie put on a clean, wash-faded nightie and went to bed early. She looked at Marva sleeping in the bed they shared and she wept. How could she deny her baby a better life than she could ever give her. When she was grown up would she drive past and feel contempt for her mother, living in the yard and hanging her clothes on a piece of string? And if she didn't let her go, how would she feel later when Marva saw all that her father had and knew that her mother had kept her away from it.

'Hush Ellie, doan' take on so. I know it hard girl. How you to give her up? How you to keep her? Hush girl, we born under a curse. Jamaica woman born under a curse. All de lovin dat we have get abused in us. Hush Ellie, you frighten me now.'

An animal was screaming in Ellie, tearing her apart with sharp, white teeth, pulling her head open and snarling behind her closed eyes. Marva whimpered and threw her small, rounded arm across the pillow. The curls around her forehead were damp and a few beads of sweat gleamed on her small top lip. She was so small. Ellie was afraid. Afraid that he would be stronger than her. He said that he would take her to court if he had to. Ellie knew that poverty would never win a court case. She hated him, hated his nice wife who wanted to do the right thing.

The next day Ellie could hardly move. She stayed in bed and a neighbour took care of the baby. Ellie felt bruised and empty. Mama came in with a small suitcase. She was brisk and businesslike.

Ellie did as she was told. Raymond came round, quiet and self-assured. He spoke politely with Mama. He only wanted what was best and so he had arranged for the court to make a decision. Mama heard him out. No, Ellie wasn't home. She had taken Marva and gone. No, Mama didn't know where they were. Then she got angry with him.

'Sake of you I loss both me daughter and me one gran chile. If you did really want was to do de right ting why you neva offer to help her support de baby, or help her get a decent job. You only wanted was to do a selfish ting, to tek her for yourself and leave us where we are wid nothing.'

Mama stormed and wept. Raymond listened. She knew where

17

they were alright, but she wasn't saying. Raymond felt beaten. The weight of her anger and love backed him into a corner. He remembered suddenly his own mother. She hated the yard they lived in and she had pushed him every way she knew how to get him to move out and to move up. Now that was love. And yet. He sent her money every month and stayed away. It was part of an unwritten contract they'd both bought into and now, faced with Mama's anger, he felt shamed. He thought of the calculating sham of his own marriage and felt another sort of shame.

They both fell silent in the small room. Raymond looked outside and saw a straggly hibiscus with a lone bloom on it. His blood and his life seemed to be hanging there in one frail blur. He got up slowly and went away.

The More You Look

The clerk was cool, above it all, the long lines, the afternoon heat. A Sunday School primness hung about her.

'You need some identification.'

'But,' he said, 'is dat I come here for.' He turned slightly and addressed the next person in line. 'Is here you come for ID?'

'Yes,' answered the man and he turned away as if to signify that he was not associated with the youth. The clerk had taken the opportunity to start dealing with someone else.

'Excuse me,' he said gently, 'I've come for my ID. If I had one already I would not have come.'

The clerk sighed, 'But your department should have sent a letter identifying you, then we could issue you with an ID.' The youth was quiet, still speaking in a simple, precise way.

'Then I must be the best person to identify myself because I know that I am me. If someone else says I am me, why is his word more true than mine?'

'Look,' said the clerk crisply, 'anybody could walk in and say they want an ID. You must have a letter from your department and that is that. Next.'

The youth stared at her as she turned away. It was as if he had eaten all the flesh off the language when at last he spat the words out.

'Raas claat.'

The line straightened up, watchful.

The clerk abruptly lost her grasp of standard English. 'Me say, you need a letter to identify you, but if you come back in here wid any of dat slackness you still nah get none.'

She snatched the next card held out to her and rolled it briskly into the typewriter. The youth straightened his tam, edged his tall body past the waiting line and walked off into the afternoon. The line of University staff closed ranks as he left.

At the big downtown garage the posh cars waiting to be serviced are all parked inside. A sort of gleaming stillness hangs over them, the BMWs, the Mercedez Benz, and the new Volvos.

'Cho, when you got you Volvo, you Visa an you Video, you gone clear.'

Stepping in from the noise and dusty traffic of the street was to step into another world. Money, money, money lined up broad, stately and quiet in the garage. The battered old VWs, the lopsided, dented Anglias, Minis and other such automotive flotsam lay dustily out in the street parking lot.

A young fellow, perhaps sixteen years old, stood in the doorway gazing in. His eyes were large, dreamy, but his shoulders were tense under his scruffy T-shirt. He approached the Works Manager slowly. The Works Manager sat in a sort of mesh wire cage to the right of the parked beauties. He was large, brown skinned, speaking nonchalantly into the telephone with his elbows propped up on a desk littered with order books and bills. His creased shirt just about encased his large belly and only just cleared the waist of his sagging trousers. The boy hung about waiting for the man to finish his conversation. The man hung up the phone and barked suddenly at the boy.

'What you want?'

'I looking for a job sah,' said the youth.

The man smiled without humour. 'You . . . but what you can do?'

'Everyting sah, everyting. I been a apprentice for tree years. I can fix automatic transmission . . .'

The man made an unpleasant noise at the back of his throat and the boy came to a halt.

'We nuh have no job for no likkle boy like you. Look how you stay. How you could be looking job. When last you bathe. You

20

no know say you mus fix up yourself before you go to people place.' The Manager suddenly became aware of a customer waiting to settle her bill. He didn't recognize her as one of his big-time customers but then, one never knew these days. He turned on the charm.

'May I help you Madam?'

The boy walked off slowly, his gaze lingering on the rows of cars.

'You have to do what you can for these youngsters,' said the Manager with great affability. 'You know, put them straight. How is he going to find a job looking like that.' The customer's non-response unsettled him. He wanted her to believe that he meant well. 'I feel sorry for them you know. But they can't do anything. If you don't look carefully they would be tiefin parts off the customer's cars. I tell you this country can't get anywhere while people having so many children all over the place.'

The woman paid her bill and went out to extricate her battered old car from the street parking lot.

'The more you look the less you see. See that airport . . .' The Dominican taxi driver is referring to the airport miles away from the capital. 'Nobody wanted it there in the first place. But what happen. This English man owned the land. He know he can't stay on there forever being as everyone talking independence. So between he and the Foreign Office (he get his good price) the English say, the airport must go there. And you know how the English stay. If they want to do something they goin push it down your throat anyway, no matter how you sayin you aint want it. They push it down your throat anyway. So at last, since Independence, we get the new airport, where it should be in the first place, near the capital.'

The taxi, with four passengers, is bouncing its way across the island to the now almost unused airport. The driver makes a few stops to deliver mail, but, for the most part, the roads are deserted. There are so few houses the clumps of banana and citrus trees must tend themselves. A pearl grey dawn hangs over the mountains, rivers appear at almost every bend.

'You see this piece of road here?' The taxi driver has a warm, easy-going voice. There is a miserable, rutted piece of road, a sheer drop to the river on one side, mountains on the other. 'Is taxi drivers clear it. Yes I tell you. It had a bad landslide, the road was completely blocked. We had to drive miles out of our way through the Carib reserve. Eventually now we organize to come and clear it. At first it was hard going and some police came to stop us. You can believe that? But we keep on and some people from down at Marigot came to help us. The police came again to stop us, but when they saw that we were serious, they started to help us and we all got the road clear.'

A few people appeared on the road. A family of soft looking Carib Indians. A man with three scrawny dogs setting out as if for a big hunt. Silence, soft mountain quiet, not even bird calls in the still morning. The road started going downhill towards the coast. Round a bend, a sudden sweep of beach and a tall man stepped out of the sea. He stood for a moment, poised between sea and land. The whole world was his at dawn on a Dominican beach.

The airport looked deserted. In the bathroom someone had scrawled, 'Who in the airport looking like a stuffed crapaud?' Someone else entreated, 'O worship the Lord in the beauty of holiness'. On the toilet door the assertion that 'God is not a black man'. Beneath, in a different hand, 'He is not a white man either'. Pious graffitti before a pee. The more you look the less you see.

The woman rushed into the police station.

'Whey Stevie? I hear you arrest him. But what him do?'

The policeman at the desk looked bored.

'Stevie?'

'Stevie Sutherland,' said the mother and mopped her face with a spotless handkerchief. In the dimness of the police station, it seemed suddenly too white. 'I'm his mother, Agatha Sutherland.'

The policeman was young, his gaze flickered indifferently over the middle-aged woman. 'Im is a bad bwoy.'

'But what him do?' The mother persisted. 'Im not bad. Is you decide in your mind say him bad. Just cause you hear say bad bwoy ina dat area. I have a right to ask what you holding him for.'

Two policemen emerged from a room at the back of the entrance office. Between them they were holding a thin youth of about eighteen years old. They walked quickly past and disappeared into a narrow corridor. The mother seemed paralyzed.

'Stevie,' she whispered and then she heard his screams.

'Mama, Mama!'

She stumbled down the corridor. His screams came faster, tearing through the dingy walls. As she drew level with a doorway she could see the two policemen holding Stevie and a third was hitting him with a hammer, on his feet, in his ribs. The mother screamed and they bolted the door. She was like a crazed animal, she beat on the door, threw her whole weight against it. On either side of the door the mother and son screamed and screamed. The policeman from the front desk came and took hold of her.

'Shut you mout an come outa here,' he said, still with that flat, bored expression. Then his face seemed to soften, his expression sweeten.

'Dem bad bwoy must tek dem licks,' he said.

Stevie's screams stopped abruptly. Only the mother's sobs filled the room. She could not get any information; she was ignored. Eventually, exhausted, she went away and started phoning. At last she got to speak to an acting Superintendent. He would not give her any information but finally promised to check into it and see that the boy went to the hospital, if there was anything wrong with him.

Agatha Sutherland went home to her one room. Anger and impotence raged through her and she sat silent as the people in the yard talked about Stevie's arrest. What had he done? No one knew. It was nearly dark when Agatha remembered that she had made a potato pone to take for her brother Alvin who was sick in the big public hospital. Wearily she wrapped up the pone and went out. At the hospital she tried to tell Alvin about it.

'Oh God Alvin, me one son. What I must do? I just can't believe dis terrible wickedness what I see wid me own eyes.'

Alvin tried to comfort her. 'Hush me love, don' tek on so. We will think of something, hush now. Any road, me will tek time see if dem bring him here then I will send word an tell you.'

It wasn't much but she left the hospital feeling a flicker of hope. The acting Superintendent had sounded quite nice on the phone. At least if they got Stevie to the hospital nobody could beat him up there. It would give her time to try and borrow some money to pay a lawyer.

She lay awake the whole night wondering how, where to get some money. The world was suddenly a place without hope, without possibilities. She was alone and the few people she knew were no better off than herself. She kept hearing her child screaming, screaming her name and she knew what it was to want to kill someone. She wanted to kill those policemen. She wanted them to die, to have their wickedness buried under the ground.

Agatha spent the next day on the road. No money, no way to get help for Stevie. She heard that there was a Government place that would investigate. But what was the use, it would take a long time and nothing would come of it for they just used the same police to investigate themselves. Agatha decided to try the Government office anyway, but first she went to the hospital. Alvin was in a terrible state. He was a chronic asthmatic and he seemed on the verge of an attack. The words could hardly come out of his frail, wheezing chest.

'Agatha, dem bring him. Wait, wait nuh. From morning me a sit over by dat window, see it look down pon de entrance. Well, me see when a police car drive up. A policeman get outa de back seat an haul out a boy. Yes, yes is him but me could hardly recognise him. De police had was to hold him up, him look so weak, like he couldn't stan up. De policeman what was driving, get out an kinda stretch himself an de two of dem stan up dere wid Stevie for a few minutes. Next ting . . . hold on nuh Agatha

. . . me a try fe tell you . . . next ting, de driver one look pon him watch an say, "Mek we go, we done tek him go a hospital". De two of dem laugh, shove back Stevie into de car an drive off.'

Later that day Alvin got an old newspaper to borrow. He needed something to take his mind off Stevie. He lay on his bed and read the paper slowly and gradually he began to notice something. He turned back to the front page and began to read again. 'Man shot while resisting arrest.' A man who attacked the police with a knife was shot and killed early this morning. There were four such reports in the same newspaper. Alvin couldn't breathe, his chest was filled with a black fog. People knew, people knew that these things were happening, yet no one did anything. Every day there was a story in the newspaper. People had stopped noticing. Alvin gasped, he must get some breath, he must call the nurse, he thought he was shouting but only a whisper was coming out. 'Oh God, Stevie, you won't even be in de newspapers, de police na go report it. A whole life can' end up so . . . not even a few words ina newspaper. Not even a few words dat nobody notice . . .'

Somewhere in the hills a group of boys end a football game. It is getting late and the sun glimmers darkly on their sweating backs. For a brief moment they stand, etched in gold against a sunset sky. Somewhere at dawn a man steps out of the sea and claims his world.

Night Thoughts

She was reading of larks singing and country girls dancing in summery English meadows. The scent of cut hay brushed past their muslin dresses and one of the girls paused to pick a spray of pink roses and lay it along her flushed cheek. In the dairy a woman churned cool, white milk into butter, another brought an apronful of apples, glowing a boisterous red, into the farm kitchen. The men left the harvest in the late summer evening and walked to the farm house to drink long glasses of cider.

All the wars that lay behind them in history had been transformed into heroic legends. The clash of battles transmuted into crests, woven into tapestries which hung far away in grand manors and turreted castles. Best of all, the age of the miserable realist novel had not yet begun. Ah, the softness and fragrance of those long gone English summers weaving their spell in books propped open by this child in a cold, Canadian winter evening, or that boy, retreating from the harsh Bombay glare to a cool corner of the verandah, and that girl on a Caribbean island, slowing her reading to savour more fully the turn of the churn which pulls up smooth, yellow butter from the milk.

And so it was that somewhere else became more real, more vivid than the jasmine blooming just outside her own window and happiness seemed to be an English summer day always beyond her grasp. For the Indian boy, who years later became a doctor and wore fine woollen suits and settled his family in Sudbury or Dorking, on that shaded verandah he had experienced a sweet happiness which he could never recapture in the neat English gardens and rows of grey houses with chimney pots thrusting into the starless nights.

For the girl on the Caribbean island, the steps into womanhood went by so quickly and always she was plagued by a sense of, this is not how it's supposed to be. She did not know either just how it was supposed to be but she stopped reading gentle books and entered the modern world of realism, of books that were like films that were like newspapers that were like paintings, so much of it hard edges and sharp, brutish colours. The realism moved to her own streets as the bars and grilles went up over the faces of the houses shutting out each other, shutting in the hard won material possessions, shutting out the stars, the full moon which shines now more clearly from the pages of a book picked up by a man, settled comfortably in his house in Sudbury or Dorking as the cold March winds whip through the streets. He swims in the warm Caribbean sea, at night he meets the woman and walks close beside her under a clear, starry sky and he knows that he can be truly happy with such a woman, in such a place.

The Caribbean woman sat in her room and stretched her arms. Tomorrow, another day in the office, but tonight she saw that the orchids on her verandah had bloomed. She brought them indoors and placed them on a round table covered with a fine, linen tablecloth which someone's aunt had embroidered. She never did like orchids, they reminded her of her father's funeral. A large bouquet of them, incredibly intricate patterns with strange colours, browns, mauves, yellows and here and there an outrageous bright pink against the dark box, slipping now into dark earth. The lowering into the earth was an illusion. The coffin with its crown of orchids slid noiselessly into a secret place to be consumed by the crematorium fire. A man lived, then was silent, covered with strange blooms as he moved into another world.

In Dorking or Sudbury, the Indian doctor hung his fine woollen suit carefully in his bedroom closet and sank wearily into bed. He had bathed with his usual meticulous attention to detail, still the smell of the hospital hung over him. He thought about his patients, working-class English women who disliked him. He would have to tell this one that she must have a hysterectomy, that one that she had cancer of the cervix. Rows of perished reproductive organs waited for him each day in the ward as cheerful nurses swished curtains around and took temperatures with no regard for the collapse of tubes and wasted ovaries which lay hidden, secret inside the women until he would reveal them. Charted and enaemaed they lay ready for his probing knife. They were all so pale. He hated that first incision when the blood welled up dark against the skin. He couldn't rid himself of the idea that each woman he touched grew older at that exact moment. His colleagues rated him a fine surgeon, he was saving lives. He curled his arm around his pillow and moved his face away from the window where the streetlight cast a sickly yellow glow against the net curtains. He couldn't sleep. He pictured the children at home who would be happy to have Ma back from the hospital making tea, putting fish fingers and chips on plates and drawing the curtains against the dark. Waiting for Dad to come home from the factory, they would watch telly dimly aware of her clearing the plates, scraping globs of ketchup into the sink. He saw her putting the children to bed and climbing into her own bed, beside Dad, her scar covered with a Marks and Spencer's nightie.

He couldn't sleep. His youth had hurried along hospital corridors and shut itself away in libraries. Grey streaked his thick black hair and his body felt soft, flabby. His English Indian children slept in their room where cool colours climbed the wallpaper, interrupted here and there with posters of rock stars who looked savagely down at the sleeping children. His mother was coming to live with them soon. She was too old to live alone in Bombay. Would he get to know her now, he wondered. In his childhood she was always busy, supervising maids or organizing her work for the many charities she supported. In the evenings she emerged on the verandah briefly, soft and scented, ready to greet his father. He hadn't known them at all.

It seemed to him now that he had always hurried past the people who he might have known. His patients only knew him by the generic name, Doctor, and he only knew them by their diagnoses. He shifted his position and gazed at his wife sleeping curled away from him right at the edge of the bed. Did she feel the need to protect her own ovaries and tubes from him? He must be crazy to be thinking like this. He stared at the flowers on the wallpaper. They reminded him of something, yes, yes, the garden in Bombay, clumps of pink flowers by the wall. Now what was their name? He couldn't remember, or perhaps he had never known. What the hell did it matter. He didn't know the name. Perhaps his mother would know. His mother was coming and she was a stranger to him.

As the Caribbean woman turned the pages of her book, he had an image of her. A woman, somewhere far away, in a room with a table covered with a linen cloth. The image was somehow consoling. He loosened his grip on the pillow and fell asleep.

After her father's funeral, she thought about happiness, what makes it, where does it spring from, why does it seem to be another place thing, like the people always setting off from her island, off to somewhere else where that happiness thing can be found. It was not something she could discuss, the word had become so unfashionable, a calendar word found now only in the racks of cards for Happy Birthday, Happy New Year. Once she fell in love and she thought that that was happiness, standing on the street watching him walk up towards her and everything was wonderfully sharp and clear and she had never seen that street before even though she went there every day, never seen the women sitting on the pavement with their baskets overflowing with fruits and vegetables, the plenty of it, the round fat richness of it. But he was a very intelligent man, he lived in America where people knew such things and he said that there was no such thing as love. It was a bourgeois fantasy and women who clung to such fantasies would be forever unhappy.

She resolutely put away the other place happiness and looked carefully at the world around her. The beauty, the poverty, the betrayals, they bloomed into strange cactus shapes. She couldn't find space to put them all and took to arranging them on paper in piles on her desk. Friends went to other countries, children grew up. Days took on an ordered quiet as age crept in through the window. Until she picked up the book. It had a faintly familiar feel to it. Ah yes, larks singing, girls in muslin dresses. The lure of the smooth, beautiful prose pictures flowed around her evening chair, the lamp tipped slightly to shed light on the small print. But gradually pictures of her own life were swimming up to interrupt her concentration.

Flashes of her childhood, young motherhood, perfection of the small ones, this one running, that one sleeping against her, small moist mouth slightly open leaving a fragrant trail of baby breath against her skin. This passionately held cause, that ousted lover, they paraded insistently through the pages. Suddenly it seemed to her that it was all real, beautiful, and the other place happiness finally did not exist.

In her home, the Caribbean woman shut the book with a small, impatient gesture, shutting out the woman churning butter, the girls in their muslin dresses, the farmers drinking cider. She could hear tree frogs singing outside in the mango tree, she could see the moon full above the mountains and a faint breeze brought the scent of jasmine in through the window. She opened the door, called in the dog and locked up the house for the night. The purple orchid trembled slightly from her bustling in the room. The door opening to admit the dog, the light switched off, the radio silenced. She went upstairs to bed. The orchid glowed in the room below.

The Bower

Her voice was cool in the hot day, it spread its way like a calm, clear lake in front of her feet. Small, slim feet but squared off at the tops and covered with powdery red dust. 'Funny how dis hard, hard groun can lif up all a dis sof, sof dust.' The dust had worked its way under her toenails and lay in well defined lines across her bony arch but stopped just above her ankles so that her calves rose up clean and straight to her small hips.

'Mawga gal . . . how you batty so big!'

'Faesty.'

That time she had gone up to Santa Cruz, her eyes confused with the shops and her ears even more confused with the noise, cars, trucks and buses all boring and shoving down the one road. Dorrie squinted in remembered disgust. But here, for now, all the flat red land rolled out quiet, accepting her dusty feet and her cool song. Dorrie stopped under a big mango tree. Ugly tree, ugly fruit, black spotted when ripe . . . 'but dat one mus ripe' her eyes widened up into the tree. As soon as she realized that it really was ripe she almost lost interest. Lazily she picked it and skinned it down to its soft pulp. 'Can't eat a robin mango skin, spoil up de whole mango.'

Flat red land claimed her again, her stride and her song renewing themselves. Dorrie walked up to the two thatch palms that stood like church wardens outside the Millers' gate. 'Bwoy, come rain or sun dem thatch stan up same way. Dem don' seem to grow any more, any part. Just de trunk straight so an de leaves spread out like a big fan.' Dorrie addressed them mentally with a rudeness that hid her pleasure in them. It seemed as if they

31

waited there, stood there, just for her to know them. They were the goodbye to the six miles between her home and theirs and they were the morning to the Millers'. She stopped and looked under the hedge for the clump of leaf of life. She crushed two leaves in her hand and used them to wipe away the mango juice from her mouth and hands.

The Millers lived in a good sized three roomed house with a wide verandah in the front. Deep pink wash covered the walls except where the red dirt had seeped its way up at the bottom. Their front garden was a mass of all the things she liked best, spidery lilies, purple and pink bougainvillaea, sour orange trees, and best of all, a white coffee rose that Mr Miller kept pruned to a smooth, round shape. Dorrie's casual gaze belied the fact that she was checking them, making sure that all her different 'roses' were in their usual place. A dirt path, worn hard by years of feet, led up to the front step but Dorrie had to take a detour and pass close enough to brush her hand on a coffee rose, to gaze into the dark, shiny greenness of their leaves.

'Mornin Mistress Miller.'

'Who dat, is you Dorrie?' way from out back of the house. 'Come tru me love. You hot nuh?'

'No Mrs Miller, I leave early and tek me time.'

Dorrie and Mrs Miller looked at each other with the warmness that was specially theirs.

'Mrs Miller, I sorry to hear bout yu fader.'

'De Lord giveth an de Lord taketh away.'

Dorrie sat on the wooden bench cotched up on the back verandah and waited for the half known eulogy. She loved to hear the words come slipping softly out of that small, round mouth. Mrs Miller had a tooth missing at the top and her words came out very sibilant through the gap. Dorrie listened and watched her fat fingers plunging and rolling in some Johnny Cake dough. 'I know plenty people said him was a hard man but him was a upright man. Him never owe nobody nutting in all him years. Even dough is long time I's a big grown ooman is plenty times I have to feel tankful to him. But Dorrie see me runnin me mout so . . . look over on de ledge you see a jug of

32

Seville orange. Pour a glass no.' Mrs Miller chuckled in the back of her throat. 'Cho, pour two, I need a little coolin meself.'

In the back room there was a cabinet with glass doors revealing rows of clean crockery. Dorrie passed reluctantly over the 'good' glasses with their ornate gold patterned rims and reached for two 'drudging' glasses of plain heavy glass. The Seville orange drink was in an earthenware pitcher covered over with a clean, white linen doily fringed with glass beads to hold it in place. Dorrie held the cover in her hand for a second, cooling her palms on the little glass beads.

'Whey dem all gone?' she asked.

Mrs Miller used her chin to point behind her. 'Dem back a groun. Hope dey remember to get de red peas an some nice big sweet potato mek I fix up a pone.'

Dorrie felt the saliva round the back of her mouth. 'Is so much tings you goin mek Mrs Miller?'

'Sure girl. But wait, in all you sixteen years you never go a wake yet?'

Dorrie shook her head, ashamed. Never known death. Seen plenty new things born, pigs and calves and kids but not even one death. Mrs Miller's tiny eyes looked anxiously over her high rounded cheeks.

'You never seen a dead person yet?'

Dorrie lowered her large black eyes and shook her head again. She could hardly get the words out, 'No mam'.

'Anyway,' Mrs Miller dusted her hand vigorously, 'de burying finish away wid.'

Mrs Miller looked closely at Dorrie. For a young girl she was always so composed. She didn't know yet how pretty she was with her slender body and large black eyes warm in her face. Mrs Miller had a husband and three sons and under her father's watchful eye her family had grown up silent and serious. Dorrie was no chatterbox but Mrs Miller always felt somehow, in a strange sort of way, that Dorrie's spirit came out easily to her.

'What I can do?' Dorrie stood up and took the glasses.

'You want I should sweep?' She smiled suddenly. 'You know I's a terror with a broom.'

Mrs Miller laughed with her. 'So you Mumma tell me. No chile, I did a little light sweeping already, no point in no big sweeping till I finish away wid de cooking. Blow up de fire mek I fry dese Johnny cakes.'

Dorrie stirred up the coals and stooped down, dress tucked between her legs, to blow the coals red.

'Aright, aright Dorrie, no bodda pass away yuself wid all dat big blowin.'

Mrs Miller put on a large dutch pot, poured in a generous stream of coconut oil and waited for it to heat.

Dorrie looked out past the flat dirt yard, past the water tank, out into the soft, hot day. Fruit trees and flowering bushes hid the Millers' ground and out back of that the grass pasture where they grazed their cows.

'Funny ting, sometimes dis whole St Elizabeth seem to be de hottest, driest place on God's land. Odder times seem as if everywhere you look is greenness an growin.'

It was getting towards that time of day when the whole earth seemed to stop and wait, quiet as quiet for midday to come. So many people all over the world would stop and look out and just hold themselves quiet for the sun to stop at the top of the sky. A strange, ancestral sun homage, an acknowledgement that the sun made the day and the life and the blood warming round your face.

Mr Miller and his three sons appeared suddenly. Dorrie's eyes, blinking to focus against the sun, saw them as only four dark shapes coming up the slight incline that led from the ground. She was sorry they had come, these four, dark, uncommunicative men.

'Mornin Dorrie.'

'Mornin Mr Miller, Donald, Samuel, Isaac.' She rolled the names out like a school rota. Each must be acknowledged by name so as not to offend. The men leaned their machetes up against the back wall and Isaac, the eldest, hauled out a big enamel basin from underneath a makeshift washstand. Samuel went to the tank and brought back a bucket of water. Silently they stripped off their shirts and washed. Dorrie seemed to watch

34

them from a long way off. The red dirt, soaped and resisted but soaped again, rolled off. Samuel watched her watching them and suddenly smiled. Dorrie started and moved away quickly into the house. Such a burning feeling in the bottom of her stomach.

He saw her looking at them, looking at their backs where the skin went shiny with water. Their backs had suddenly revealed that they were not one collective male body but four distinct male people. Four very different backs belonging to four faces that she had always grouped as one.

Samuel had smiled at her.

'Cho, what mek I stan up dere like a fool. Cho, why I never did start layin de table or somethin.'

Dorrie was so angry with herself that she stood halfway between two rooms not knowing what to do next. She, her, she whose days had always moved calmly and purposefully into evening and turned up again at day. School in the week and church on Sunday. Her Mama milking cows and keeping house. Sewing baby dresses to send to Santa Cruz market every other Saturday. Her Mama never quite got over her disappointment at having only the one daughter and kept herself reminded of her failure by sewing for other women's fruitfulness. Not that her Mama sewed in bitterness, she took pleasure in the daisy chain embroidery, the hemstitched edges and the tiny little pink and blue buttons. And not that her Mama bore her – Dorrie – any bitterness, she loved her and cherished her and brought her up a good Christian child. But this failure of her Mama's ('Oh is only the one daughter yu have? Oh my, yu don have no boy pickney?') had eventually made her refuse men her bed.

Dorrie could remember, when she was very small, a man who used to come often to the house. She would go to bed and leave them talking and laughing around the table. Once, much later, she had asked her Mama about him but she had laughed and said, 'Cho, I too old for all dat foolishness.'

What foolishness? Dorrie, plaiting her hair in front of the mirror had wondered. Now she knew. It was foolishness looking so at Samuel's wet back. Baptized like a baby at the church font with the Sunday afternoon sliding away outside.

She could hear them talking outside with Mrs Miller. Where could she go? No, she must stay and help Mrs Miller with the wake. Her Mama was coming over later, and many more people from the district, she couldn't just run away so, just like that.

Dorrie went out to help Mrs Miller. Johnny cakes and saltfish and Seville orange drink all lined up already on the table. They all sat down and Mr Miller blessed the table. The meal began in silence. Dorrie could not, not if she had been sinking in the swamps, she could not lift her eyes up from her plate. She could only stare at the flat, pink ceramic roses blooming under the saltfish until her eyes felt as if they were rolling out of her head and lining themselves up beside the flowers. Two large black flowers blooming on the plate.

'Yu get any sweet potato?'

'Umm hmm,' an affirmative grunt from Mr Miller.

'Lord have his mercy!' declared Mrs Miller dramatically and involuntarily.

Dorrie's eyes left the roses. She knew!

'I don't have no coconut.'

'Mama,' sighed Isaac, 'you don' remember Miss T over de shop sen you two for some cassava?'

Mrs Miller breathed a sigh of relief and laughed at herself. 'Cho, my rememberance leaving me these days!'

Dorrie giggled and relaxed enough to look around at the men.

'Yu want me shell de peas?' she asked.

'Who tell yu we get any peas?' Samuel teased.

'Well I jest hope yu get peas because yu can't mek peas soup without no peas!'

Donald, the youngest, who was only fourteen, started laughing and spluttering into his orange drink.

'Hey I bathe already,' Isaac pretended to be angry at Donald for spurting juice on him. Dorrie looked at Samuel, the pain in her stomach eased off and she laughed.

'What a way oono happy, we supposen to be in mourning.' Mr Miller killed the laughter and gloomily masticated on his saltfish.

Mrs Miller sighed. 'Cho, leave dem man. Dem is young, mek

dem have a little brightness no. Any road Papa gone to heaven, I sure of dat so we shoulda feel happy for him.'

But it had gone. They finished their meal quietly and the men went off to sleep.

At last Dorrie had something to do. She was sat down with two big enamel basins, one for the peas, the other for the empty, curled up pods. She rolled a pod in her hand and the peas fell pinging in the basin. Mrs Miller put some big beef bones into the soup pot and set it on the fire. Mrs Miller washing up the lunch plates in a big yabba, Dorrie shelling peas into the basin, they chatted about harvest service coming up, about good crops and bad crops, about Miss Harvey the pianist and how she did those special roll arounds at the bass of the piano for 'Bringing in the Sheaves'. The peas went into the soup pot then there was coconut to grate to make coconut milk for the pone. They had to set up another coal pot to set the oven on. Dorrie knew what to do. She was busy. Sweat sprouted under her armpits and trickled down inside her loose cotton dress. 'Lawd it hot.' Mrs Miller paused for a minute to fan herself with the hem of her dress. Dorrie looked at her plump, black knees and her fat thighs joined together. She thought sadly of her own thin, straight thighs and for a second she longed to be plump, all joined together at thighs and bosom, upper arms meeting against soft padded sides, sweat having to ease it's way between the two instead of running freely down her ribs.

'Well sir, I don't know what I would do without you today Dorrie.'

Mrs Miller was on her feet again. 'Miss T up de shop did help me wid de fish yesterday, good frien better dan money.'

Dorrie sat on the bench grating coconut into a big tin tray.

'What a good life,' she thought, at peace with Mrs Miller and the new afternoon coming on.

Mrs Miller took the tray away from her. 'Chile you nearly fallin asleep. Come, before de men wake up, go a de wash stand and tek a little coolin. Yu bring yu frock?'

'No Mrs Miller. Mama had was to finish it fe me, she goin bring it later on.'

With a towel and soap Dorrie washed as best she could in the basin. Mrs Miller produced a tin of 'Evening in Paris' dusting powder and Dorrie stood still while she smoothed the heavy fragrant powder on her back. Again Mrs Miller wished to herself that she had had a daughter, a daughter growing into a woman with her body all fresh and young like Dorrie's. 'Go ketch a minute on de sofa. We finish down here fe now.'

Dorrie was fast asleep drifting over flat, scrubby plains baked red in the sun. Evening, starry cool, wrapped her in her dreams but when she woke it was only late afternoon and the house was humming with activity.

A few men had arrived and were constructing a bamboo bower out in the yard and they were already laying palm leaves for the roof. How had they done it so quickly? Dorrie marvelled at it. A bower for a wedding, a bower for dying. She never saw them practising, yet they knew what they were doing.

'Yu don' practise for dying neither,' Dorrie suppressed an irrelevant giggle. She saw Samuel's body bent over making a bench, all curves and straight lines like the bamboo. She turned away quickly.

Mrs Miller was trimming lamps. 'Come Dorrie put out some soup dish mek we feed dese hungry men.'

'Den Mrs Miller, what we goin eat tonight?' Dorrie asked.

'Fish an bammy an plenty bread, I fix dat up from yesterday, all cover up in de cupboard. An I grind up whole heaps a coffee for de drinking. Some of dem big time singers boun to bring some rum to wet dem throat.' She glanced towards her husband who was well out of earshot. 'Jest hope him don go on too strict like . . . you know,' and she smiled anxiously.

Dorrie served out big plates of soup while Mrs Miller went to lay out her dress. She felt adult and important and kept filling up empty plates as fast as she could. The men washed down the soup with great gulps of water and talked quietly among themselves, talk of Mrs Miller's father, other wakes, other bamboo bowers. They were well pleased with themselves and belched appreciatively as they left Dorrie to finish their work. Dorrie wished she could help them, join in somehow, instead of being left with piles of greasy soup plates to wash. All those peas she had shelled all washed down in somebody's stomach and only greasy plates left. Dorrie washed up and started in with the serious sweeping.

Dorrie plaited her hair and went out to watch for her mother. She could hear Mrs Miller splashing about with water in a basin, then later, she could hear the rustling and groaning of her satin slip unwillingly settling around her hips. Dorrie stood by the coffee rose tree looking out for her Mama.

Evening was coming in quickly so it was her voice she heard first, talking along her steps. Mama was walking with Brother Ezra, the big time church singer. All week he sat hunched up in his little tailor's shop, sipping his rum and water and making overalls for the bauxite workers up by Nain. But come Sunday he seemed to grow out of his hunched up position and spread out and up into a big, thick set man with a voice flowing out deep and rich from under his carefully pressed dark flannel suit.

'Mama, yu bring me frock?' Dorrie almost hissed.

'Hey!' Mama jumped in surprise. 'Lawk, Dorrie I never see you standing dere. Me heart jest a poundin, poundin ina me chest.'

Dorrie put her arm around her, 'Sorry Mama, I never mean to frighten yu, but time getting on an I still in dis ol crush up frock.'

'Evening Dorrie,' Brother Ezra reproved her.

'Evening Brother Ezra, evenin Mama, tank yu for the frock.' Dorrie clutched the paper parcel and ran inside.

'Mrs Miller, what a way you look gran!' Dorrie stopped short and gazed at the transformation. Mrs Miller tried not to be pleased.

'Cho, de frock so ole, time I tek off some a dis fat.' But she sneaked a quick look in the mirror and patted her sequined bosom. 'Dorrie it not too tight?' Dorrie looked her over carefully, surprised that Mrs Miller could doubt her good looks. 'Oh no Mrs Miller, you look jest like a queen.' Mrs Miller raised her plump chin, patted her hair firmly into place and sailed out to meet her guests.

Dorrie shut the door and quickly changed into her white dress. It was a simple dress with a wide skirt and a collar that stood away from her long slim neck.

'Mama still meking me look like a little pickney.' She wished she had a purple dress with sequins. She posed in the mirror as Mrs Miller had, chin up, eyes proud . . . but she still felt like a schoolgirl, so she compromised, with some more Evening in Paris down underneath her dress. People were gathering and talking in little groups, their faces gleaming dully from the light of the kerosene lamps and their shadows independently peopling the walls of the verandah. Mr Miller and his sons appeared. Dorrie's eyes searched for Samuel. Long sleeved white shirt, tie, hair brushed and brushed to form a soft cap around his face. Dorrie and Samuel looked at each other and smiled but Mr Miller was talking.

'Let us begin with a prayer for the departed.' He said each word very carefully and they all realized that it was the signal. They filed into the bower and took their places. Old faces and young faces, plump faces and angular faces, all beautiful with a sudden group composure.

Mr Miller droned and intoned. The group said many 'Amens' and many 'True, true ting' and even a few 'Praise de Lord' but Mr Miller flowed on like the river Jordan. Dorrie looked for Samuel in the family group, his eyes were only half shut and for a second they slid towards hers but quickly squinted tight shut. At last Brother Ezra was called upon to lead the singing, red Sankeys flew open and 'Rock of Ages' filled the spaces round them. Dorrie joined in, wondering for the first time about some of the words.

> Naked came to thee for dress
> Helpless look to thee for grace
> Foul I to the fountain fly
> Wash me Saviour or I die.

The words made her feel extremely uncomfortable as if she really were naked. 'Wash me Saviour or I die.' What did it mean? Why should she feel naked and dirty. Thank goodness they were rolling on to 'Oh God our help in ages past'. You could really lay your voice into that one. She specially liked the line 'Time like an ever rolling stream'. Mrs Miller seemed to have read her thoughts and her high soprano soared up and up into an improvised descant. They sang on and on. The older people sinking deep into words like 'blood', so many in the hymns, and making little gasps before special words like 'Saviour' and 'Prince of Glory'. By the time they hit 'Nearer my God to thee', Dorrie's voice was hoarse and beads of sweat stood out on her forehead. Sure but every time Samuel said the word 'nearer' he seemed to be moving right across the heads and singing mouths, he seemed to be drifting down right inside her mouth, down to the very start of her singing.

Dorrie moved quietly out of the bower and flopped on the verandah step to cool off. The sky, the land seemed vast, borderless after the intimate closeness of the bower. Mrs Miller came out and went into the pantry to bring out the coffee. Samuel materialized on the step beside her.

'You can surely turn a good tune,' he was talking to her.

Dorrie looked away, up in the sky pinpoints of light and shapes and patterns. She wished she could disappear, suddenly just not be there, be somewhere else with a definite shape, a place. Samuel unfolded a startlingly white handkerchief and held her face towards him. He patted her forehead, her eyes, her mouth gently with the handkerchief and Dorrie gratefully breathed in the hot iron smell of the handkerchief, relaxed and smiled at him. They stood up and walked away from the singing and the kerosene lamps. Samuel put his arm around her waist and she put her face on his shoulder. What happened to all the flat red land at night? How was it dark, where was the redness gone, where were the smells of the daytime? For a minute she was frightened, everything familiar had left her, the landscape was not hers but changed, shut away from her in a night darkness. Then she remembered Samuel bending over the bamboo poles, why it was all part of the scheme of things, quite natural, curves and straight lines, dark and light, beginnings and endings, some things are always known, others are only gradually revealed.

Roots

'Hi Mass Tom, what a way you cotch up comfy ina de cotton tree root. De tree na go fall down if you move, you know.'

Mass Tom grudged her a half smile and said nothing. Marthy regretted having tried to be pleasant and moved on quickly. 'Dirty ol big pants man, never do nothing all him life.' Marthy switched her thoughts to a more constructive vein. 'Well, some of us have tings to do an de morning done past nine o'clock.' She glanced briskly round the morning, and satisfied that everything was in its place, she hurried home.

As always, Marthy slowed her step as she came to her gate. Her little house glowing pink and blue always pleased her. Every square inch of her property was used. Hot pepper, sweet pepper, beans and peas, Irish potato, sweet potato, yam. Marthy frowned at her tomato plants; they looked sickly and spotty. Reminded her of the agricultural expert who'd come around. Told them to grow one crop and sell it for a good price instead of growing little, little all around. She kissed her teeth in new vexation remembering his schoolified voice.

'The experts has done whole heaps of tests on this soil and tomatoes is just the crop for this area.'

Marthy popped off a dead leaf and crumbled it in disgust. Just as well she had only planted a few. The fellow so stupid. What was the point of growing whole heaps of one thing to go an hassle yourself to sell it to get money to turn around and buy the very things you could grow yourself? 'Then suppose now,' Marthy mumbled to herself, 'just suppose I did plant out tomatoes an they never thrive. I woulda did end up wid no money an nothing to eat neither.' Marthy kissed her teeth and pushed open her door.

She eased her comfortable frame into her 'straight back' chair. He'd given her that. Funny dreamer man he was. Twenty years ago she was twenty, plump and firm and bursting with energy and independence. He talked so much nonsense about Orion and the Big Dipper, yet in the end she would listen to his voice spark up about Jupiter and Mars. Even now she would look up quickly some evenings to catch a first glimpse of the evening star. He came from nowhere. He stayed long enough to cut logwood posts for her fence, to build on another room and to paint the house all her favourite colours. He left after Venus' first birthday. Marthy sighed. Venus would be twenty today and she was all the way in Kingston. Seems like she'd been gone three years instead of only three months.

Marthy sorted out her pile of straw and chose two suitable lengths. She just hoped Venus was being sensible and not taking up with any sly-eyed old man like Mass Tom. He well past fifty and still trying to feel up the young school girls. She started on her basket and the irritation she felt at Mass Tom translated itself through her finger into the sharply moving straw. 'Men,' she muttered. 'Even when dem don't have no looks nor intelligence dem still think every woman mus love dem.' That type had laughed at Dreamer Man. Said he must be a batty man to stay at home all de time and go on so quiet. When he left they said it was Teacher's sixteen-year old son what took him away from Marthy. Was it him? She wasn't ever sure but she preferred to think it was just his need to be on his own again that had taken him off. Marthy felt for sure he hadn't gone to another woman or started life in another Venus. In the evenings when the sky settled abruptly from pumpkin, orange and tangerine into the deep starapple colour of night, she had looked for him. He was coming and she would wait.

Her straw clicked up again. She was thinking of all those poor women all over the place, hundreds and thousands of dry backyards, washing in pans under breadfruit trees. Washing men's clothes and babies' clothes. Different men's clothes every

43

year but the same babies' clothes as they passed on down to baby number five, baby number six, every new baby a new hope that this man would stay with her and treat her good. Such a simple and universal hope that remained so universally unfulfilled.

The creamy straw slowed to a gentler rhythm as Marthy gazed into the blue eye of a morning glory. That was it! No root. Morning glory has to hang on to something to grow and pretty though it is it can't last long. The morning glory was struggling up a pear tree. See that now, thought Marthy, a good strong root that can keep feeding itself and growing itself into something strong and special. That was Venus' pear tree, her navel cord buried under it when it was just a little clump of green leaves. A shining feeling spread itself inside her head. 'See that now.' She addressed her absent Venus, 'You just remenber you lovely an strong like dat pear tree an no bodda mek no Mass Tom fasten on to you.'

'Miss Marthy,' dumpy foot Eeda was calling over her fence, 'letter from Venus down Post Office for you.'

'Tank you Eeda, I soon go for it.' Marthy tried not to rush, sorting out her straw and slipping on her shoes.

How comes everybody know she got a letter from Venus. They wanted her to read it out, right there in front of the Post Office. But Marthy said she couldn't stop . . . 'Pot a fire, I can't burn out me good pot. Yes, yes me will tell you bout it tomorrow at meeting.'

Marthy hurried off. Shower of gold was bursting from the sky. 'Dat a real lovely tree anyway you look at it,' she thought. For telling that lie she set herself a penance. She would really have to set a pot on the fire before she could read the letter. Gungo peas. She would have to pick them and shell them and pound the escallion and it would take her quite a while before she could open the letter. She saw the letter propped up on the table waiting for her to finish shelling the peas and she would pretend to be harrassed . . . 'Cho Venus, you don't see I busy. I soon come to you, jest wait little no!'

Marthy held the envelope crisp in her hand. She slowed her

step, he was still there. But it must be after twelve and the sun was burning down on him.

'Mass Tom, you sick? How you still a jest sit so into de cotton tree root?' Mass Tom was sweating, his down-cornered eyes glimmered up at her.

'Miss Marthy, lower you voice do.'

Marthy went closer. But wait, he really did look sick. For a second she thought of all those girls he had left to sweat in labour. 'I shoulda jest leave him dere like an ol goat,' she thought.

'Miss Marthy,' he pleaded like a sick child, 'come here no mam, help me, do.' Marthy went closer.

'Come, let me help you up.'

His eyes were swimming down his cheeks, 'Miss Marthy, I hitch up ina de tree, I can' move.'

He was half-lying, half-sitting between two large curving roots, but there was enough space for him to move, surely. She held out her hand and clasped his wet palm.

'Come man, heave up a little, heave up yourself.' But she couldn't move him. Marthy felt a shiver of irritation. 'What wrong wid you any at all? Hol on mek I get Desmond from de shop.'

'No, no,' he whispered. 'Don't call nobody, run get a cutlass.'

Her eyes dilated in horror. 'What you want me do wid a cutlass Mass Tom?' The stain of sweat broadened and spread around his shirt.

'Miss Marthy, some roots growing outa me into de ground, dem pulling me down.'

'Lord you sick bad,' she dropped down beside him, 'come mek me . . .' But as she tried to put her arm around his waist she felt something hard and rough, something like a root growing out of his back and disappearing into the ground. Her stomach heaved and she had to lean against the cotton tree.

'Mass Tom,' she was surprised to hear her own voice, 'I going for me cutlass. Try keep moving so more don't grow.'

His eyes were closed and the tears dripped back into his hair.

45

'Dem grow already, all down me legs, all up me back, from me shoulda . . . don' leave me Miss Marthy . . . don' leave me . . .'

He was moving quite quickly now. As he went down his body shrivelled, like a leaf, like a large, dry leaf crumbling into the ground.

He was gone. Her mouth was dry. She looked around quickly. It was a joke, he was behind her, somewhere. Marthy got up and looked around the tree. No, she knew she had seen it. 'Lord have his mercy,' she said, backing away from the spot. It was smooth, dark, brown dirt. Not in the least unique, just dirt.

Marthy felt a pain in her hand where the crisp edges of the letter had dug into her palm. She rehearsed in her mind's eye her morning, her routine morning. Her walk to the Post Office. She saw herself holding the envelope . . . 'Mass Tom, you sick? How you still jest a sit so into de cotton tree root?' Marthy walked home. What had she seen? Why? Who would believe her if she repeated such a tale? She held the envelope tight against her breast. 'Venus, you mother going mad in her head. Help me Venus.'

She stopped at her door. But she had closed it. She saw his back in the straight back chair, she saw his hands working on her basket, the straw moving smoothly. He turned as she came in and smiled into her face.

'Morning Miss Marthy.' She smiled at him and pulled out the chair opposite.

'I got a letter from Venus,' she said.

'Is that right,' he said. 'Read it to me, no?'

She smoothed out the envelope and opened it carefully.

'Dear Mama and Dreamer Man.' Marthy looked up. 'How she knew you was going to be here?'

'I don't rightly know,' he said, 'but go on reading eh.'

'Dear Mama and Dreamer Man,

Hope you are keeping well. I liking it here . . .'

46

The Virgin

London in the early sixties. What a place! What a time! Jamaicans there studying, the lucky ones on scholarships or supported by money from 'home' were full-time, the rest worked and studied part-time, everyone was studying something. Black was beautiful as the Jamaican men were discovering through the eyes of girls with names like Gita and Elke and Brigitta, sexually liberated au-pair girls with wonderful bodies and long blonde hair and oh so un-clinging, so undemanding. It was all heaven.

Three of the guys shared a flat in Fulham. It was a haven for a little group of students, particularly those living in inhospitable hostels faced with a coin in the slot for a hot bath and sludgy, lukewarm meals that smelled of boiled cabbage. They would gather, usually on a Sunday, to eat chicken and rice and peas and listen to the latest ska and Millie, tiny, cute little Jamaican, making the charts with, 'My Boy Lollipop ... You Make My Heart Go Giddy-up'. The London trio had Jamaican friends studying in other cities and, from time to time, one or other of them could be found installed at the flat, escaping the provinces or the serious enclaves of Edinburgh, to spend a weekend in London where it was all happening. These sons and daughters of a new, aspiring middle class were optimistic, ambitious and intensely nationalistic. No one doubted for a minute that he or she would go back and make a difference. It was pre-Vietnam, pre-Biafra, a never to be had again time of innocence and faith.

The guys played hopscotch between their regular Jamaican girl friends and the changing collection of Brigitta's and Ulricke's. Girls who were not girl friends but a sister or a cousin of someone, would come and go, finding a place until they established affairs outside of the group and finally dropped out.

Moira was someone's cousin. A slim, dark serious girl of eighteen, studying music at the Royal College. She spent all her time in those draughty music rooms, her fingers wedded to the black and white piano keys. Only on Sundays, when the imposing door with its heavy brass door knob was firmly closed, would she drift down to Fulham to hang out with the other Jamaicans. She would laugh at the jokes, listen to the ska and rock but there was something tense, apart about her. If any of the boys passed an exploratory hand along her slender neck or tried to engage her in a too personal, too sensual conversation, she would smile and change the subject. Among themselves, the guys called her 'the virgin' and they would plan strategies to catch her, lay bets as to which one would relieve her of her virginity and introduce her to the real world. But as time passed and there were so many agreeable, available girls, they accepted her as a sister and even developed a certain protectiveness towards her.

The flat had three bedrooms upstairs, a bathroom on the landing, a living room and kitchen downstairs. Like most London flats it had no central heating, so during the week the boys lived and studied in their rooms, finding it easier to keep one or two rooms warm at a time. One bitterly cold afternoon, BT (everyone had long forgotten what the initials stood for) a resident, and Stewart, a regular visitor from medical school in Edinburgh, were alone in the flat. They were in BT's room, Stewart propped up in bed studying, BT tackling a pile of ironing, for the price of the boy's popularity, or perhaps one of the reasons was that, in this land of scruffy students, the Jamaicans still believed in a clean, properly ironed shirt. Men did not do such women's work at 'home' but these boys would have surprised many a maternal eye by their assiduous attention to hygiene, to cleanliness and to the properly ironed shirt.

BT was a dark, muscular fellow who, in spite of his weight-lifter's physique, was lifting nothing heavier than trial balances, income and expenditure reports, in his accounting class at the Polytechnic. While others would look at the larger picture, consider serious questions like, will the West Indies win the test match against Australia, BT would quietly remark that there was an Australian in his class who always wore red socks. It didn't matter what colour shoes, or what colour trousers he wore, always the red socks. At first Donny or Patrick would pause and ask him, 'So man, what the hell that have to do with the test match?' But after a while they began to appreciate his ability to register and ponder over the small idiosyncracies of life. BT had another talent. The man could cook chicken and rice and peas that would throw the entire sensory system into high gear. First the smells, and he didn't believe in hurrying his masterpieces, so the smell would hover around the flat for hours, growing more intense as the afternoon wore on, while the saliva flowed and the gastric juices pumped in anticipation. Then the sight, the chicken roasted golden brown, redolent with seasonings, bursting with stuffing and at last the taste, the rice and peas cooked with liberal amounts of coconut milk, permeated with the taste of an unburst country pepper perched saucily on top of the gleaming, steaming mound of rice.

Stewart was a tall, slim half-Chinese Jamaican, able to put away prodigious amounts of food and generally accepted as the 'brains', the most serious and mature of them all, perhaps because he had a steady girl friend and laughed at the others juggling their love lives. To hear them tell it, a legion of Aunties was forever arriving from Jamaica. Patrick on the phone to Ulricke . . . 'No, Donny isn't home right now, had to go visit an old aunt up from Jamaica.' While of course Donny was busy upstairs with a new conquest. Or Sharon would come knocking and be told that Patrick was working late at night at the library when, of course, he was over at the pub gazing deep into Elke's lake blue eyes as under the table his hand found the smooth plumpness of her fair Scandinavian thigh. The trouble was, the boys were too kind, too dedicated to duty. The world was full of women needing to be pleasured and they had discovered to their horror, from whispered pillow stories afterwards, that the world was full of men who did not like women, who when faced with a joyous, generous woman were so inept, even cruel, as to leave them tense and unhappy. Faced with this knowledge how could the guys not rise to the occasion, how could they not spread the joy, how could they fail to fulfil this mission, reassuring women that they were beautiful, desirable and that their contented, satisfied smiles were the only goal of these men who loved women.

On this bitterly cold Thursday afternoon, BT answered a knock at the door and was surprised to find Moira standing there, eyes streaming, nose red, her whole body trembling.

'Come in girl, we're upstairs in my room, only warm place in the flat.'

Moira followed him upstairs and stood just inside the door, a pathetic, frozen figure. BT went downstairs to make her a cup of tea and she stood, still in her coat and boots, hunched up close to the small paraffin heater which threw a wavering light and heat into the small room. Stewart looked at her over his book.

'That bad is it?' He sounded like a full-fledged doctor already. 'Come, take off your coat, take off your boots and don't stand too near to the fire, you'll get chilblains.'

She did as she was told. He held back the cover on the side of the bed nearest the wall. 'Get in,' he said. She climbed clumsily over him, still in her bulky sweater and corduroy pants. She curled up there in a small, trembling ball.

'Stretch your feet out and try to relax,' he said.

The sheets were cold, particularly at the bottom of the bed but, obediently, she stretched her legs out. She tried to lie still but she was shaking violently.

Stewart lowered his book and looked at her carefully. Her face was turned toward the wall but he could see the shine of tears on her cheek.

'What happen Moira?'

'I came second in the recital,' she said between chattering teeth.

He dug into a pocket and found a handkerchief, clean but crumpled and smelling of eucalyptus from a half-empty packet of throat lozenges which had been in his pocket for days. The smell reminded her of a time, long ago when she was a very small girl and had gone home with her friend Lurline. She lived with her grandmother who had white hair plaited in a crown on top of her head, very white against her dark skin. When she was leaving, the grandmother said, 'Come here my little sweetness,' and she hugged Moira against her bosom. She was so soft, so warm and she smelt of eucalyptus from a handkerchief she had tied in a knot and tucked into the front of her dress and Moira wanted to stay there forever, leaning against her and being her 'little sweetness.' Shortly after that, Lurline went away to live with her mother in New York and she never saw them again, her best friend Lurline or the grandmother with the white crown and the smell of eucalyptus.

She pressed his eucalyptus handkerchief hard against her closed eyelids. Stewart was saying, 'That happens. Next time you will be first.' He sounded so certain about it but he didn't understand. When she discovered music, it was wonderful, she could be at the music teacher's house every evening after school and most of Saturday, so she hardly had to be at home and as long as she came first and won prizes, they would leave her alone.

BT came upstairs with the tea. She thanked him and sipped the hot, sweet tea. She did not like sweet things, but it tasted good and she liked the heavy, warm feel of the ceramic mug against her palms. Stewart reached into a bag beside the bed and fished out two aspirin. He seemed to have everything organized about his person or close to him by the bed.

'I don't like taking tablets,' she said, trying to reclaim herself.

'Tough,' he said. 'Take them. They won't do you any harm and you might just be coming down with a cold or something.'

She swallowed the aspirin with noisy gulps of tea. She was never sick, she never cried, but she had to hold the cup carefully as another wave of shivering caught her.

Stewart took the empty cup from her and stretched over to put it on a table near the bed. He had barely moved from his half-seated, half-prone position in the bed.

'Take off that heavy sweater,' he instructed, 'you'll get too warm.'

51

She didn't want to, she remembered that she was wearing a shapeless, old cotton T-shirt underneath, but he held out his hand for the sweater and she took it off. He reached over again to put that also on the table and she burrowed down under the covers.

BT was pressing on with his shirts. Stewart returned his attention to his text book. The only sound in the room was the iron moving across the fabric, a page being turned. The heater threw a flickering, round pattern on the ceiling, like a paper doily put under little iced cakes at tea time when one visited with Aunt M, thought Moira. She drifted in a half-sleep remembering strange fragments. Learning to dance.

She was about ten years old, sitting on the verandah of her Aunt's house. She was a tomboy, an expert tree climber, a swing upside down from one leg kind of climber, always scruffy in shorts. But today she was wearing a dress, sitting on the verandah so it must have been a proper visit with the adults inside somewhere talking. She had a long, thin scar on one leg from climbing under the barbed wire fence on a dare, over to the neighbours to pick hog plums and her hands full, her cousin had hissed that the man was coming out of his house. He held up a piece of the barbed wire but let it go in fright when the man's voice came closer and she was almost through, just her left leg coming through last. She mopped herself up and wore her only pair of trousers for a while, so as not to have to face any questions about how she had come by the gash in her leg. And now, sitting there in a dress, she examined it closely, long, thin, paler than the rest of her skin and she decided that it was altogether a very satisfactory scar.

Uncle was from Panama. He put a record on the gramophone and the horns and drums and guitars washed over her and she got up and stood by the french windows looking in at him dancing to the music and he came, took her by the hand and started teaching her the cha-cha-cha, then the merengue. He was patient and soft-spoken, an effortless dancer. She tried too hard, she was too energetic and he had to slow her down, teach her how to listen to the music, how to let the beat of it come up through the polished wooden floor where patches of sunlight lay, come up into her feet at the same time that the sound was coming through her ears down towards her hips so that when they met, hips and feet would reach a secret understanding and know how to move in exactly the right way. But there was a second understanding that had to come between the man and the woman so that the beautiful senorita could follow his lead at the same time that he was leading, her steps a mirror image of his. The horns and drums and guitars flowed out of the garden and the colours and light of the garden flowed back into the music and round her small child looking into the adult self.

One Christmas, at about the same age, her father came home in the full spirit of Christmas. Three men were with him and noisily they set themselves up on the verandah in the wooden slatted chairs and after the rum was served they started playing and she and her two sisters ran to sit on the verandah steps and watch them play and listen to the songs.

> 'Kitch come go to bed
> I have a small comb to scratch you head.'

They thought it very funny and their father was laughing with them and swaying his broad shoulders in time to the music. But their stepmother came, banished them from the verandah and said something to their father about what kind of music was this to be bringing into the house. She shut the doors to the verandah but the music and the scratchy old voice reached them, imprisoned there in the living room and Aunt P, who was very tall, very, very tall, and often had a sweet rum smell about her, must have been similarly banished, because she joined them there.

> 'Where did the naughty little flea go
> Nobody know, nobody know.'

Aunt P, so very tall, sang the words and laughed and they laughed with her at the song about a flea and they copied her movements, winding from the waist, little backsides flicking every which way, shoulders shaking, non-existent bosoms thrown out, for in that they were also her conspirators and would help her hunt for her foam rubber falsies when she was rushing out on a date. Such badness and laughter and natural sexiness 'wining'* to the Mento band.

She was twelve years old, tall and thin and she was sent to spend a year with her maternal grandmother in England. On the banana boat going there, to England, she had seen, day after day, the vast, empty horizon and she had been afraid in this first absence of trees and sun. Moira hoped that her Grandmother would be like Lurline's lost Grandmother, but she was not. She was short and plump with thin grey hair wound in a little bun at the nape of her neck. She was German and spoke with a foreign accent even though she had lived in London for a very long time. Moira liked her, but the trouble was, they could find nothing to talk about.

Moira did not know her mother, this German Grandmother's daughter, she had left Jamaica when Moira was a baby. This Grandma did not know Jamaica. She lived in a house in Notting Hill Gate and rented out flats to African students, keeping the top floor flat for herself. She had a German daughter-in-law who lived nearby and occasionally they would visit her. Daughter-in-law gave Moira little marzipan sweets made to look like miniature fruits and there was nothing to do while the two women talked but eat marzipan apples and pears. She had a boring little son who she petted and adored and talked about endlessly as if he were not there beside her hanging on to every word.

Grandma was a good cook and coming in from the coal dust smell of a winter afternoon, she would find a heaped plate of food ready for her and afterwards a sweet biscuit from the Peek Frean tin. But still they could find nothing to talk about and Moira could not eat anymore and so the odd year passed between them.

The flat had a perfectly good bathroom, but twice a week Grandma would haul out a large, zinc tub, set it near the fire in the living room, fill it with hot water and proceed to take her bath. On bath evenings, Moira would stay in her bedroom,

* Way of dancing and rotating the hips.

ostensibly doing her homework, but more often looking at the shadow plays going on in the houses behind theirs. There was a young couple who used to argue, facing each other by the window, and she would look across her back garden, across their identical back garden, and see them clearly in their third floor flat. He waved his hands when he talked, so she assumed he wasn't English. The woman would thrust her face forward to make a point then draw it back in, like a turtle. Sometimes she would walk out of the frame and he would stand at the window alone, looking out into the night. London was so silent, full of silent people, everything so grey and damp that she wondered what they found to talk about so animatedly. She envied them, wanted to be in their flat with them, with the crowded furniture and the crowded wallpaper like those flats she saw, peering through the lace curtains of ground floor flats on her way to school. But when the man stood alone like that, staring out at the dark, at the sky that had no stars, she shivered inside herself and looked away.

One evening, Grandma had finished her bath and called her in for tea. The room was warm and moist. The bath tub with its grey, soapy water still stood beside the fire while an old-fashioned waltz played on the radio.

'Child,' she said. 'Can you valtz?'

'No Grandma,' she said.

'Come, I vill teach you.'

And so she did. They started off sedately enough, Moira a bit wooden at first then getting the hang of it, Grandma, so short and plump in her old bathrobe, light and energetic on her feet. They whirled round and round, gathering up speed, very lively, Tales of the Vienna Woods and the water filming over in the tub. When the music stopped, Moira helped her empty the tub and she was sorry that it was over.

At the end of that year, she sailed back home, like a dark little bird flying south, and she puzzled about that year, trying to understand what it had all been about, only that evening learning to waltz, came back to her clear and warm out of the grey, cold silence of London. By the time that she was a teenager the cold had grown all through her. Faced with the agony of teenage parties, she no longer knew how to be natural, she could not dance, she was the tall thin shadow by the wall.

Moira was warm, all over her body and her mind seemed to float up from a far distance, a little nearer to being awake, but she did not want to wake up. she wanted to lie there forever. She had turned and her face lay against the side of Stewart's chest, against the soft wool of his sweater. His hand was against her skin, moving in small, slow circles in the small of her back. The circles threw a pattern of heat out, through her whole body and the centre of the pattern was a hot, liquid feeling at the pit of her belly and she seemed to be moving there in small circles and the circles were moving in towards each other, closer, tighter and suddenly the hand stopped and everything inside her stopped and waited. The unbearable waiting held her until at last she opened her eyes. The heater threw its paper pattern circle on the ceiling, a lamp by the bed cast a glow on the text book. The ironing board was folded away and BT gone.

Suddenly there was a banging of doors downstairs, talk, the TV switched on, the others had come home. Stewart shut his book, got up and left the room. She lay there for a while, aware of her own body, the ribs here, the waist here, all of her soft and small and warm. Slowly she moved her head, dark was shut up outside the window. She got up, put on her boots and sweater and combed her hair. She wished she could just drift out through the window and not have to face them all.

Donny was in the living room, changing the programme on the TV. He looked up as she came downstairs, concern on his face, in his voice.

'What happen girl? Hear you nearly froze to death. You feeling better?'

'Yes thanks Donny,' she said and her voice seemed to be coming from a long way away.

'Man it's wicked out there tonight.' He saw that she was carrying her coat. 'Where you going? Stay nuh. You could sleep on the couch.'

'Thanks,' she said quickly. 'Wish I could but I have an eight

56

o'clock with the Professor tomorrow morning and my notes, which I haven't even looked at yet, are back at the hostel.' She was intrigued by this voice which was not her own yet knew what to say.

Donny still looked concerned. BT came in from the kitchen where he had overheard the conversation.

'I'll spring you for a taxi then,' he said firmly.

'Hey,' she laughed, touched by their concern. 'It's OK really. There'll be lots of buses around.'

BT ignored her protests, called a taxi and pressed a pound note in her hand.

'You probably not looking after yourself,' he said. 'Too wrapped up in all that music stuff. And don't feel any way if I tell you, you're too skinny for this weather. You need to put some flesh on those bones.'

'Yes Auntie,' she said, mock serious. 'Thanks for the tea, BT.'

They laughed at the silly rhyme.

Stewart came downstairs as the taxi was pulling up outside. He went over and helped her on with her coat.

'Take care,' he said. He smiled but his face was inscrutable.

'Bye,' she called, generally, to everyone. 'Thanks for everything.'

She hurried out, got into the taxi and disappeared into the cold, dark London night.

Burnt Hill

He arrived in Burnt Hill at the beginning of July, parked his old truck under a guango tree and started building his house. The village had heard that old Sam Davis' land had passed to his grandson but it had lain fallow and dry for eight, ten years and the grandson had never even come to look at it. Now here he was, in the middle of the July heat, just arrived and starting building with hardly a word to a soul. He had bought a quantity of supplies with him and all day long and far into the evening they could hear him sawing and planing, preparing his wood. He turned up at the rum shop one night. Didn't have much to say for himself except that he wanted a youngster to help him for the next few weeks. They discussed it in the shop for a while and suggested he get Miss Robbins' big boy Marcus seeing as he was going to the new Technical school and should know how to handle himself. It was arranged that someone would send a message and Marcus would show himself the next day.

When he left they puzzled about him for some time. Leonard Davis was as unlike his grandfather Sam Davis as mutton is to pork. Sam had been an easy going man, friendly with everyone and content to live his life simply. His wife Miriam, now there was a woman. She had a back as straight and hard as a church pew and a terrible, fierce ambition to go with it. When their three children were high school age, she picked up and took them all off to Mandeville and from that day on she was finished with Sam Davis and Burnt Hill. Said she wanted higher education and something more out of life for her children. Sam used to go to see them every now and again and take a good sized crocus

58

bag full of whatever produce was in season at the time. His friends marvelled at him. As his good friend Simon Harris said . . . 'If I did have a hard face woman like dat leave me, I woulda say "tank God fe Jesus" and fix up meself wid a nice young gal.'

Sam ignored them and continued his visits to Mandeville, but it seems like his family were getting very high tone for they started sending the maid to meet the country bus and relieve Sam of his crocus bag of yams and cassava. So gradually the visits dwindled and he spoke less and less of his family. As the years drew on he used to hear occasionally from a daughter who lived in England, and when he died, his son and other daughter from Kingston came to bury him. They had arrived, very pleasant but very citified and it was clear they, neither of them, would be coming back there to live.

Now here was Leonard Davis, a big, strapping, young dark-skinned fellow, not citified like his father, but not friendly either like old Sam Davis. Heavy and quiet, just arrived and started building. Marcus, having been accepted for the job, was questioned but could say very little. Seems like Leonard was building a simple enough house but he was very fussy with it. Everything had to be just so. He was even renovating the lattice work from Sam's old cottage. Marcus had felt strongly enough to intervene at this point.

'But Mr Leonard why you don' trow way dat ol someting. Better you get some a dat new grille work to finish up de verandah.'

But Leonard had persisted and when they had stripped off the old paint and sanded it down, Marcus had had to agree that it was fine workmanship and it looked good on the new verandah.

The end of August came as hot and dry as July, but the house was growing at a great speed. Malcolm Jones, who ran a small shop which sold odds and ends of hardware, seemed to be the only person who had actually spoken more than a few words to Leonard. Not that he was unfriendly mind you, more that he kept himself to himself and got on with his work. Malcolm had taken a walk over there one day and reported to the rum shop

59

later, that it was a nice enough house but very old-fashioned. Wooden floors and sash windows and goodness knows what else that took time and trouble to make.

Malcolm was a bit of a handyman in his way and he took to going over some evenings to help out. He liked furniture work and they would sit in the yard of an evening, sanding down some of the old furniture that had been lying around in Sam's house. One evening they were working on two straight back chairs when Leonard asked: 'Who lives over there, in the blue house?'

'Oh, dat's Mrs Harris' house. She keep de basic school but she gone to Kingston since school give holiday. She told de children say she was going back to school herself but she soon come back. Why you ask?'

Leonard shrugged. 'Nothing. I just like the house. I wondered why nobody was there.' He paused to get at the inside of a chair leg. 'So, where is her husband?'

Malcolm laughed. 'He gone way long time. Well, you know here is too country for anybody wid a little education and ambition. Sooner or later dem pick up an leave. Mek it worse, dem was married five, maybe six years an all she try she couldn't mek a baby for him. Well it happen dat him get a coolie gal pregnant. De next ting we know, him up and gone to Sav-la-Mar. Set up house an business dere wid de coolie gal.'

After he left, Malcolm put away the tools and sat for a long while looking into the cool darkness. He had inherited about three acres of fairly flat land and a derelict house. But there was a good-sized water tank, a big guango tree and several fruit trees. The land adjoining his was smaller and slightly hilly but it was thickly planted out and also had its own tank. It was a shame that everything there would die from lack of water. The next evening he walked over to the blue house, found a bucket by the tank and started watering. It was slow work with only the bucket but he moved methodically through the front garden and started on the back. What must have been a vegetable garden was only limp, brown stalks but she had a row of young citrus plants struggling to stay alive. Leonard emptied bucket after bucket of water on them and listened to the slight hiss of the water going into the dry earth and smelled the strong, warm smell that rose from the wet earth. There were two large pots of ferns on the verandah and he hesitated a moment before pushing open the little gate, going up the three steps, and watering the ferns.

August turned into September and not a drop of water fell from the open sky. Burnt Hill seemed determined to earn its name as even the customary night dews seemed to have stopped and the land rolled out red and dry every morning. The farmers, who were famous in the rest of the island for their dry-weather farming techniques, had mulched their plants carefully and accepted the dry spell as part of the order of things. But Leonard was aghast at it, it seemed to him that some great force was witholding something simple, effortless to give. He was amazed at the painstaking way in which the farmers carried water out to the plants, just a little trickle for each as the level of water in the tanks grew lower and lower. He took to going over to the blue house every evening to water the plants. He didn't think about it much, he wanted the plants to survive and he liked the small, blue-washed house. He admired the gingerbread carving over the doors and he liked the simple squareness of it on the hilly plot of land. On the evenings when Malcolm came, he didn't go. One evening Leonard started over and stopped abruptly. There was a light. So she was back. He felt curiously angry, turned and went back to his house.

Burnt Hill took on a new look in September. Children appeared in groups, starched and khakied, going to school. The rains came and the men and women who had seemed half-dead in the still, heat of July, unbent, moved as if released from some ancient frieze. There was digging and hoeing and planting. Voices calling, snatches of song moved in the still air. Leonard felt the movement around him and he too set to work on the land. Almost imperceptibly the evenings came earlier and then there was not enough light to work on anything.

One evening, Malcolm came over. He had heard of a fine mahogany felled over at Topside and he had bought a few pieces. Working on the furniture had renewed his interest in wood and

61

he thought he would make something himself, but there was enough if Leonard wanted a piece. Leonard said yes, he would buy a piece to make a table. They disagreed mildly over possible designs. Malcolm was all for an ornately carved table with curved legs. Leonard preferred a simple oblong with straight legs.

'Mrs Harris have a fine old table. I help her french polish it one time. You know dose ole time table wid a pedestal an de legs dem curve an end wid sort of claws. You know de one I mean Leonard?'

'No,' Leonard said.

Malcolm wouldn't let it drop. 'How you mean "no". You don' meet her yet? Seeing as you is neighbours, I surprise at you man.'

Leonard shrugged, 'Cho Malcolm, you know I'm not one for visiting. I'll meet her soon enough. I'll come over to the shop tomorrow to pick out that piece of wood.'

Leonard spent the next morning designing his table and working out the dimensions. In the afternoon he went over to the shop and waited for Malcolm to finish serving ice pops to a group of school children. Malcolm's shop was a one-roomed affair but he had enclosed the side verandah and there he kept stocks of odd things like nails, shoelaces and paint. The last child was ushered out clutching his tube of bright green ice and the men were just about to go through to the verandah when a woman rushed in.

'Evening Malcolm, hope you have some kerosene, don't know how I've run out already.'

She was small, slim and her voice was low, rushing out from her small frame.

'Evening Mrs Harris. You in luck, truck coming tomorrow but I have a little put by you could have. But stop, I don' think you know your new neighbour. Dis is Mr Leonard Davis.'

'Evening,' they said and there was a silence as they looked at each other.

Mrs Harris broke it.

'I've been admiring your house. I hear you built it yourself.'

62

'Thank you,' Leonard said, 'Malcolm helped me with the furniture.'

'Oh,' she sounded interested but Malcolm was handing her the kerosene and she was paying, saying goodnight and hurrying out. Leonard chose his wood and walked home slowly.

That evening he sat on his verandah and looked at the blue house. He wondered how the garden was doing. He could imagine her now, active, quick hands planting a new garden. He had imagined that she was old, an old woman teaching other people's children. But she was not old. Older than he perhaps but not more than mid-thirties he guessed. She was pale skinned with dark hair, colouring that Leonard found strange, unattractive even. Quiet and the night came early and he sat there feeling a flicker of restlessness. He needed his books, a radio perhaps, he wasn't sure why he had been delaying going into Kingston to fetch his things. The pattern he had established of working on the house had completely absorbed him, but, he thought, stretching lazily, it was time to make the trip into town. He would go the next day, get it over with. If he went like that, mid-week, there would be nobody there. He could simply pick up his two boxes and leave the key with the next door neighbour. He would not have to face his parents and their aggrieved comments, the small guilt-making jabs, 'after all they had done', giving up his job, 'such good prospects', to hide himself away 'in the depths of beyond', as they put it. And, of course, he could not explain. He could not say that the prospect of working to buy things did not interest him, of drifting into a marriage, much like theirs, did not interest him. It was all sound, solid, and it frightened him, the years stretching ahead, known even before they had happened. He wanted to make something very simple, very different, for himself. He could not explain because they were so proud of having lived out Grandma Miriam's dream, to be educated, professionals, a far remove from Grandpa Sam, travelling in on the country bus with his country talk and his bag of yams.

By the weekend he had his few possessions unpacked. In the evenings now he had company and as September grew full and wet he would sit and play his guitar. He played all sorts of music,

music written years before and some never written but passed along the generations like a great fishing net, drawing in and giving out as it moved through time. Sometimes he played his own music, haltingly, then finding the thread he wanted, repeated, woven together and finally noted down. In the blue house, Mrs Harris heard the notes dropping wetly in the September evening. She wasn't sure if she liked his being there or if she slightly resented him. In the afternoons she would see his dark, heavy body moving slowly between the rows he had dug. He might be a good builder and a good musician but his farming looked rather pathetic. She couldn't see even a smudge of green starting in the red earth.

One Friday evening she came home from school, bathed and changed and for the first time in years, felt the weight of the weekend stretching heavily in front of her. She went out to the garden and saw with pleasure the feathery green tops of her carrots. She stood staring at the soft, small leaves, remembering all the other years she had planted, the excitement when they started growing, the despair when drought or floods or insects threatened to leave her with no crop at all. Slowly she went back to the house, fetched some newspaper, a small shovel and started digging up some of the plants. Wrapping them carefully in the paper she set off towards his house. Dusk was edging into the sky and wisps of pink cloud floated there as if they had snatched their colour from the red land.

In front of his verandah she stopped. There was no light in his house and she turned quickly to go away, but he was coming through the doorway.

'Evening,' he said.

'Evening,' she said and her voice hurried on. 'I was thinning out some carrots and beans. Planted too many this year. You want some seedlings?'

'Yes,' he answered. 'Thank you.' There was silence and she felt she hated him. Could he not say something? She held the parcel out and he reached for it.

'Thank you,' he repeated, 'though I don't seem to be much good with them. None of mine have even sprouted yet.'

She felt silly, standing there in the dark. 'Perhaps you didn't get good seed.'

'Malcolm said it was good,' he said.

'His stuff is always good,' she said, sounding defensive. 'Maybe you didn't prepare the beds right. This land hasn't been worked for years.'

'I think I may have planted them too deep,' he said. 'Yes, maybe that's what I did.'

He seemed to have forgotten about her and she turned to go.

'I'll just put these down,' he said quickly, 'and light a lamp.'

He returned with a lamp, holding one hand cupped around the top of the shade even though there was no breeze to snuff it out.

'Won't you come in?' He asked with an old-fashioned stiffness.

She stepped up on to his verandah and sat on one of two chairs drawn up beside the table. His guitar was leaning against the other and he moved it aside to sit down.

'I hear you playing in the evenings,' she said. 'I can't make out the tunes from where I am, I just get a sort of outline.' She stopped abruptly and looked at him. His eyes were heavy lidded, deepset, and in the lamplight they gleamed oddly. He seemed like a large, slow cat, cautious and self-contained.

'Do you like it?' he asked.

'Yes, I like music but,' she shrugged, 'I don't know much about it.' She sounded more definite as she added, 'I like all sorts of music as long as it's not all electrical . . . you know.'

He laughed. 'Yes, I know. I do these things and send them in and, if I'm very lucky, a group will get hold of it and make it all loud and electrical. Sometimes I can't bear to hear them when they are finished. But sometimes, the group improves on it, somebody picks up on something I hadn't fully developed and it ends up being, well, more exciting somehow.'

'So you write music then,' she said smiling.

'No,' he was almost gruff, 'just tunes. But it buys me this,' he looked past her. 'Independence, no noise, no hassle.'

They sat for a long while, talking and silence in little patches until the sky was black, scattered with stars and only a small curl

65

of a moon. She got up to go and he walked with her across to her land. There was something cool and heavy between them out there under the dark sky yet at her gate she said, 'Will you come over some time and play your guitar?'

He could hardly see her face, only the smallness of her and her quick voice.

'Yes, I'll do that,' he said and watched her go into her house.

The weather changed. The days passed wet and thundery with sudden flashes of lightning. There were days when school was closed early and the children admonished to get home quickly before the rain. But they dawdled and their shrieks could be heard as they ran and splashed and held their faces up to the wet. Mrs Harris was conscious, on those wet afternoons, that she was waiting. She wished that she had never walked over there, for now she was waiting and she felt a sharp irritation with herself. One day, the skies opened just before she got home. She let herself in and tore off her wet clothes. She put on an old bathrobe, made some coffee and stood by the window watching with stiff anger as the rain flattened her plants. 'Bloody immoderate country, if the drought doesn't get you the floods will.'

There was a knock at the door.

'Yes,' she called, 'come in.'

Leonard stood there very wet, staring at her with his heavy eyes.

'I'm too wet to come in,' he said.

'Take your shoes off then,' she said. 'I'll get you a towel.'

He sat in her small room with his shoes off and mopped at himself with the towel, then she saw that he had brought his guitar wrapped in an old jacket.

She gave him some coffee and sat away from him drying her hair. It was thick and curly and as she brushed it it sprung away from her head, alive and dark. She was like that, he thought, alive and tensed up, angry at something.

'You know,' he said, 'I don't know your name. Other than Mrs Harris, that is.'

She laughed, looking at him and he felt slightly frightened of her, all her small brittleness frightened him.

'It's Mavis,' she said. 'Horrible name isn't it?'

'Almost as bad as Leonard,' he smiled. He looked around the room. 'I like this house, I used to look at it . . .'

'Why?' she asked abruptly, startled by the idea.

'I don't know, it's a simple, workable design I guess. When you were away I used to come over and water the plants. I liked it here. Only, I imagined that you were an old lady, that you wouldn't mind.'

She pulled her bathrobe more closely around her and looked at him with strangely dilated eyes.

'Did you. Thanks for doing that.' Then she laughed. 'But I am old. Old Mrs Harris who keeps school!'

He laughed then, looking into her eyes and picked up his guitar.

Outside the rain was slowing down but the sky was still grey. A grey and red landscape wrapped around the house as he played, his bare feet moving slightly to the sound. The music and the dense grey evening swirled through her head in thick patterns and she got up and started preparing a simple supper. She seemed to stand off from herself, seeing herself standing in the kitchen, aware of a soft dishcloth in her hand, rubbing and rubbing at a white cup, trying to focus away from the patterns and his slowly moving feet.

He sat, head bent, wrapped up in his sounds, hardly moving when she brought a lamp and set it on the table.

'I'm hungry,' she said. 'Will you eat?'

They ate, speaking occasionally with a curiously stiff, old-fashioned sort of politeness. He watched her clearing the table and the room felt very still after the soft rushing of her voice. He felt hot in the small room, hot and closed in with this woman. He wanted to touch her hair, touch her throat where her voice lived. When she had cleared the table she sat and said awkwardly,

'I'll put something on and walk part of the way with you. It's stopped raining. Did you notice?'

He reached out and touched her throat. 'I love to hear your voice. I wish there were notes like that I could play.'

She held herself very still as he touched her throat. His hand was so large, so rough at the tips of the fingers, it seemed separated from his smooth, cat body. It seemed to him that something waited in her. Waited tense and coiled and withheld from him. He kissed her strange face, closed like a small flower.

In the weeks that followed Leonard thought it would never stop raining. His tank overflowed and washed away all his efforts at gardening. He felt helpless against the great weight of the sky and the smaller yet equally persistent weight of the woman in the blue house. He wanted not to think of her. He worked quickly to finish the table he was making, to push her away from him with planing, with careful fitting of joints together. He wanted only to see her and take her, not to fill his days with the sharp edge of her. Sometimes, in the evenings, she would speak of her day at school. Of the children she found exasperating and of those who were responsive to learning. She did not speak of her past so their talk was often filled with other people's children, other people's doings and sayings and in the midst of it their lives stood rooted, unyielding in their separateness. But slowly he was making up his mind about her and as October came he was badgering Malcolm for more wood. He started on the last piece of furniture he planned to make. When it was finished he asked her to come to his house. She had been strange about this, welcoming him to her house but seldom wanting to go to his. She said though, yes she would come. She would come on Saturday at six.

Leonard made supper, amazed at himself for the fuss he made over it.

He watched her crossing his washed out land. The sky was full of that strong gold light that comes in the evening towards the close of the year. She seemed herself all golden and lit up as she walked towards him and took his hand. She was more relaxed and affectionate than he had ever seen her. She had put a sprig of jasmine in her hair and the room was full of its scent and their voices and the food shared on their plates. After dinner he showed her his gift and she laughed and threw herself across it.

It was a four poster bed, made in dark mahogany and she was full of admiration of him.

'But really, it's so lovely, and you made it!'

Then she fell silent and looked at him. He looked away and said quickly,

'It's for us. You must come and live here. Yes, marry me and come to live here.'

She walked round the room looking at the bed, at its simple lines and dark, glowing wood. She stopped, far from him and spoke abruptly.

'But I can't do that. I was married. You've heard all the stories. When he left I stayed in the house. I made a place for myself there. Can you see that? It was very difficult. There were nights when I cried. There were days when I couldn't get up. The house was dirty and I couldn't clean it. I was cold and barren and I could do nothing. I wasn't a woman at all. At last I grew angry. But it took a long time. I am ashamed of it. There were days when I couldn't bear to see other people's children, couldn't bear their noise and chatter and their beautiful limbs, their beautiful faces. But I stayed and made a place for myself and I can't give that up.' She paused and looked at him. 'You are young. You will find someone, start a family . . .'

Leonard heard her and his own voice came darting out into the room.

'I don't care about the children thing,' he said, 'but you must stay. I don't care about marriage if you don't want that although we are being talked about as it is. I don't want you to be talked about. I want you to stay here.'

His will was like a large, live fire behind his darting voice, she couldn't move away from it and yet she couldn't let herself be swallowed up in it either. She stood straight and stiff by the bed and her eyes held a great coldness. But he reached out and took her hand twisting it hard against his chest. They made love in a rage. They filled the bed with a bizarre almost tangible rage of love and despair.

She wept. Large, noiseless tears rolled into her hair where the creamy coloured flowers drooped close to her cheek. He looked at her then, saw the flower of her own will opening as the tears slid into her hair. He understood then, not in any way he could formulate into words but in some silent, instinctive way.

Burnt Hill talked for a while about Leonard Davis and Mrs Harris but as more Julys and Septembers rolled past the red land, as the citrus trees bloomed behind the blue house and cassava plants appeared on his land, the village looked away. They found new and more changeable topics to discuss.

The Colony

The area had once been completely rural town, residential, pleasant homes with wooden railed verandahs looking over their own small gardens to the narrow, winding street. Now, as the spirit of entrepreneurship flourished, it stood hesitant, halfway between residential and commercial, unable to make up its mind. The butcher, the baker, the furniture-maker plied their trades here in converted front rooms or, if very successful, in square concrete additions with mean little windows squinting up at the carved fretwork eaves of the old houses. The pleasant smells of planed wood and bread baking flowed into the street to be absorbed further along by the oil and grease smell of a garage where young men in dirty overalls revved up engines and generally made themselves happy fixing transmissions, changing spark plugs, inventing adaptations for spare parts that could not be found and shouting curses and instructions at the handful of ragged little boys who hung about enthralled with this masculine world of motors and wires and sumps and pumps.

Past the garage, a hairdresser and dressmaker tried to pull the street back into shape and reassert a female presence with neat signs hung over their front doors. 'Dressmaking Done Here' announced one, the other, scorning such a bald statement, declared itself 'Chic Beauty Salon'. Schoolgirls waiting to fit school uniforms at Flo's, the dressmaker, gazed enviously over the verandah rails at the women who emerged with long, gently waving tresses or startling magenta curls, a total transformation from the short, black hair that had entered the salon some hours earlier.

Most of the houses did double duty, shop in front, children, homework and kitchen in the back. On the outskirts of the town, hotels were soaring into the blue sky, tourism was the economic future, said the new breed of economic planners, fresh from University and full of facts and figures on GDP and GNP and the need to earn Foreign Exchange to improve the Balance of Payments. But here, on this street, tucked into the heart of the town, the residents did their own economic planning and organized their own balance of payments with a message, sharp or gently prodding, depending on the client.

'Tings bad dese days. Beg you settle up wid me dis week.'

'Me not making no more frock for Sheila if I don' see her wid money in her hand.'

For the most part, the residents translated the island's fifteen year independence from Britain into a personal code of independence. No longer were jobs in the Civil Service, in teaching and nursing, seen as the only stepping stones to social and economic mobility. People made their own way as independent trades people and the garage owner, who now lived in a spacious, modern house in one of the new suburbs, was considerably more affluent than the neighbour he had left behind to frequently and ineffectually protest the noises and smells of the garage which were, he said, bringing down the 'tone' of the street. The poor neighbour, struggling to bring up his family in the shabby gentility which was all that his teacher's salary would allow, had to suffer the further indignity of reading in the newspaper that the garage owner, not content with his economic superiority, was now courting social and political mobility through his appointment to the Board of the local High School, despite the fact, as the teacher brooded bitterly, that the man's education had been modest in the extreme.

The teacher had to face a yet more serious assault to his sensibilities when his wife announced that she had, quite unknown to him, brushed up her secretarial skills, and landed a job at one of the hotels. In the space of one brief, and for him, tragically unhappy year, she had started wearing high heels, makeup, and reading business journals, had been promoted to Office Manager and was now earning more money than he was.

The teacher was assailed by various maladies; migraine, allergies, impotence. His wife suggested that, since he was good at maths, he should change career, move into insurance or banking, both lucrative careers. He resented her suggestions, her wanting to help him, as if what he was doing, what he had poured all his energies, his training into doing, was suddenly a totally invalid activity. He was shamed by it and could only sit silent in front of this attractive, managing new wife, the ambitious and outspoken children growing up under his roof but turning more and more towards her for advice, for the sharing of confidences, for money, like so many flowering shrubs growing towards the light. He was a casualty of the new order sweeping the island. As a casualty his wounds festered until finally he succumbed. His grieving widow sold the house, moved into a sparkling new suburb and began, tentatively at first, herself to succumb to the amorous advances of a certain bank manager, who she was later, uncomfortably, to discover, already possessed a wife who lived in Kingston.

Unaware of this tragedy, Tom inched his car past parked trucks, a few cars, and peered into the dark street trying to understand the haphazard system of numbering. He found number forty-two, a charming old house, in better repair than its neighbours, stubbornly displaying a small, well-kept garden behind a neat wooden fence. He parked, pushed open the gate, walked up the steps and knocked softly on the door. He was about to knock again when the door was quickly opened. Claudia peered out.

'Hi, it's you. Hush, Mama sleeping already.'

'I've been sent to get you,' he said. 'Their Highnesses have issued a directive. You must come to their party.'

She looked at him for a moment, undecided, then she smiled.

'OK. I'll come. Come in, I won't take long to get dressed.'

Walking soundlessly on bare feet she led him through an unlit living room into her bedroom.

73

'Claire said she invited you, when she met you yesterday on the beach,' he said.

'Oh, Claire Smalling. Yes she said something about a party, but I hadn't planned to go. Thought I wouldn't know anyone there and, well, you know, it's difficult to get there without a car.' She motioned him to sit down, opened an old-fashioned wardrobe, looked in attentively, chose something to wear and headed for the adjoining bathroom. Tom looked around. There was a single bed with a flowered cotton bedspread and a dressing table with a small stool. He sat on the bed thinking that she must have grown up in this room, a bit surprised at its utter simplicity. He suddenly remembered another bedroom, in New York. He had been young, just married. He always woke up before her and he would glance at her from the bathroom, a crown of fair hair, all the rest hidden beneath the bedclothes. He used to wonder how she could breathe, buried like that, even in summer, beneath the sheets. He had loved her so much then, loved their long, late night talks, making love in the simple room with only a mattress on the floor and a painted bookshelf which she kept hung with her jewellery and adorned with little pots of makeup, creams, perfumes and her three Chinese boxes in which she kept letters, photos, private memorabilia from her past.

By the time his third novel was published, she was already established as a successful fabric designer and the bedroom had been transformed. He began to feel closed in by it, the heavy drapes, the colourful, massed cushions, the ornate, matched Art Nouveau mirrors. The late night talks had long since ended. She lived now in a whirl of activity, of schedules and appointments, and little dinner parties with rake thin men and women who looked, not as if they had spent all their lives in the most affluent country in the world with endlessly available food, but rather as if they had just escaped from years of famine in an impoverished, drought stricken land. They spoke in rushed, high-pitched voices so that he felt as if he had fallen out of the fashionable New York apartment into a strange bird sanctuary all glittering and colourful, screeching and darting about with their sharp beaks and dark claws.

Claudia emerged from the bathroom in a simply cut, bright green dress and rummaged around in the closet for a pair of low-heeled sandals.

'Ready?' she asked.

She was very slim, tall with black skin and small, beautifully shaped features. He thought that she looked like a Benin bronze.

'You are beautiful,' he said.

'Me?' She looked at him in surprise and then laughed. 'Shall we go?'

They walked out through the dark living room, got into the car and set off. For a moment he had felt disoriented, so suddenly switched from his memories to the sight of Claudia standing, smiling at him. He concentrated on navigating the narrow, winding streets of the town then relaxed as they came out along the coast road. A full moon hung directly overhead and the sea, silvered by it, slapped gently in on the rocks before rolling back out to gather up strength to repeat the roll back to the rocky shore. On the other side of the road cane arrows thrust their feathery heads into the moonlight, their movement in the faint evening breeze mirroring the lightly crested waves on the other side of the road.

'It's lovely, isn't it,' she said. 'I often wonder if a foreigner like you sees it exactly the same, or differently.'

'I don't know.' He thought about it for a while. 'Probably not exactly the same yet very similar. It is lovely. Not like the tourist brochures. Lovely in a way that gets under your skin.' He laughed. 'You know I was supposed to be here for two weeks. It's now a month and I still can't leave.'

'Oh well,' she pretended to be cross. 'I guess I'll have to change that ticket again,' and they laughed, remembering how they had met at the airport. He had gone to extend his ticket, she had been pleasant but cool until she noticed his name,

'What a coincidence,' she had looked at him carefully. 'I just finished reading a book written by a man with the same name as you.'

She returned her attention to the ticket. He studied her dark, graceful head, a pretty, young, black girl.

'Did you enjoy the book?'

'Yes, it was great, it was called "Standing Room".' Her face was animated and he realized that she was beautiful, that her smile seemed to shimmer somewhere between her mouth and her eyes so that he thought of afternoon lakes, of the sudden, pure note of a saxophone in a dull, crowded room.

'Read any more of his books?' he asked.

'No,' she said. 'The bookstore in town isn't the greatest.'

She handed him his ticket and looked at him suspiciously.

'I don't suppose . . .'

'No,' he said smiling. He took his ticket and left.

In the silence of the car he became uncomfortably aware of her perfume, of her long, slender legs and so he began to tell her about the Smallings. Lord and Lady Smalling, they had bought a house in Jamaica three winters ago. Lots of money, he was something or other in finance, she was endlessly sociable. Claudia had heard some of it already during her conversation with Claire but she liked listening to his low-pitched voice with its soft American accent.

They left the main road and started climbing uphill, past small farms and a few, isolated houses. At the top of the hill they turned into the driveway of an old house that had been carefully restored. They pulled up and joined the semicircle of parked cars. Two curving flights of steps with wrought iron railings led up to the front door which was flanked by enormous terracotta urns filled with flowering bougainvillaeas. A uniformed servant ushered them in and Claire Smalling rushed over to greet them.

'Darlings,' she gushed, 'how heavenly that you found her Tom.'

She led them through a large, high ceilinged room with local mahogany furniture which gleamed darkly against the highly polished wooden floor. Claire had a rounded, compact figure and she moved, like her conversation, in abrupt starts and stops, pointing out special features of the house as they walked through to the back verandah. She was deeply tanned and she wore a loose-fitting white dress which showed sudden patches of back and bosum as she changed directions in her path through the house. Her accent cut into the polish and glow of the quiet rooms like dressmakers' shears cutting into silk and Claudia felt as if she were in danger of tripping, of falling, either over Claire herself or her oddly punctuated conversation. Tom was silent.

The party was milling around at the back of the house on an L-shaped verandah bordered by a neatly clipped lawn. Claire led them over to a tall, thin man.

'Darlings, my husband Henry,' she introduced them.

Henry shook hands and smiled slightly under his long nose.

'Darling,' Claire addressed him, 'remember I told you about Claudia, how I discovered her on the beach reading one of Tom's novels, of all things, and we had such a lovely chat. I was so cross with you,' she fired at Tom, 'keeping her hidden away from us.'

Tom tried to protest but she was off again.

'Drinkies, must get you some drinkies.'

Claudia looked around. There were two or three light-skinned local couples, members of the same, wealthy, land-owner family, and a young businessman with political ambitions who had married into the family. He was flirting with a stunning looking redhead while his rather dowdy wife was having an animated discussion about dogs with a cadaverous English matron. They were both obviously having a good time. The other guests were mainly European with a sprinkling of Americans. Mid-forties couples escaping the hazards of winter and big business to play in the tropical sunshine and explore useful international contacts. The only other black people there were the waiters who eyed her with suspicious glances. Claire, who had moved ahead confident that Claudia was following her, came back to get her and tucked her arm firmly under hers. Claudia, whisked along on her impatient arm, hovered briefly like a bright green hummingbird, sipping introductions among the couples until, at last, in response to an invitation from an American couple, they drew up chairs and sat down. Lester Endelbaum was a short, balding man with a cherubic smile who patted the seat next to him with a plump, insistent hand.

'Sit, sit . . . there . . . a drink . . . good.'

A waiter haughtily presented Claudia with a drink and whisked away Claire's exhausted gin and tonic to return immediately with another.

Claire was saying, 'You did get the O'Keefe didn't you? Was sure you would,' although neither Endelbaum had had a chance to respond.

'Such divine colour. Reminded me of the garden here. I do believe I said that at the time.' She turned her cornflower blue eyes emphasized with irridescent eye shadow, towards Claudia. 'Super home they have, in Chicago of all places. I was absolutely not prepared to leave New York. Just hate, hate, hate provincial cities, but I'm so glad you insisted,' sparkling briefly at Rose Endelbaum, a dark-haired woman with fine, dark eyes. 'Such a shock,' Claire was rushing on. 'No, no, an absolute shock to find such wonderful architecture and really civilized restaurants and of course,' swamping Rose with the incredible blue eyes, 'your house is too perfect for words. Quite spoilt New York for me after that.'

'Never touch the place myself,' Lester laughed, getting a quick word in.

'Used to love it when I was just getting started, now I leave that side of the business to Sammy, my son,' he explained to Claudia.

Claire rushed off to greet a latecomer.

'What business are you in?' Claudia asked.

'Furs,' he replied. 'Wouldn't know much about that here, would you! That's why I like coming here, have to talk about something other than furs. Been my life for so long, at first I didn't know what to talk about.' He laughed, a happy, round sound at the back of his throat.

Claudia decided that she liked him, his small, plump cheerfulness.

'Do like your dress,' Rose said in a low, hoarse voice. 'Such cheerful simplicity.'

Claudia, hearing the insincerity in her voice, looked at Rose's expensive couturier clothes, the perfect matched emeralds at her ears and smiled.

78

'Thank you,' she said, and Rose, a trifle annoyed at her refusal to be insulted, impatiently waved the waiter over for another drink.

'You a model,' Lester asked. 'You would look great in furs.'

Claudia laughed. 'Oh no, I'm not a model. And to be honest, I don't think I would like furs, all those little animals . . .'

The music was suddenly turned up and the area in front of their table became the dance floor. A tall, uncoordinated man asked Claudia to dance. He stomped around in a frenzy while the watching couples stared at her smooth, fluid movements.

From a corner, Tom nursed a rum and ginger and watched them watching her. He was sorry now that he had allowed Claire to pressure him, with her detailed instructions, into finding her house, into opening the car door for her, aware of the way her legs swung over the curve of the car seat like two black exclamation marks in the middle of an otherwise unaccented piece of prose. How on earth had Claire found out where she lived?

After that first meeting at the airport he had taken copies of his other two books for her but she was on a later shift so he left them for her without a note. Some days later he saw her waiting for the airport bus and he gave her a lift. She thanked him for the books and said she was enjoying them. He believed her but there was something cool, distant about her. He dropped her at work, amused at his ruffled ego. 'Writers are not collectables here,' he had thought. Now Claire had turned the tables and was obviously about to add Claudia to her collection.

As if reading his thoughts Claire appeared and leaned against him.

'Are you sleeping with her yet?' she asked, staring at Claudia.

'No,' he said, 'not that it's any of your damned business.'

'Why not?' she asked, rubbing the curve of her breast against his arm. 'I'm just as curious about her as you are. What's it like to stroke those long, slim thighs. Chilled white wine and imported strawberries, yes that's what she should have. Up in my room with the windows open but the shutters closed against the sun.

Perhaps we would invite you, some time later. A little ménage à trois.'

'You're disgusting,' he said and moved away abruptly. He walked out into the garden. 'Poisonous,' he thought, staring at the blooms of an alamanda glowing golden in the dark garden. He shivered, remembering an evening he had spent there. They had all had too much to drink. Henry passed out on the sofa and while the servants locked up the house, Claire fell upon him, her blue eyes shining and unfocused as she led him up to her bedroom. He remembered the white shutters and the cool, white sheets. He shivered again as a quick image of his wife flickered suddenly into his mind. Other rooms, other women, a careless crumpled lust since she died.

Claudia detached Lester Endelbaum's plump hand from its stealthy approach to the curve of her arse and went to join Tom in the garden.

'Could you organise me a lift home?' she asked. 'I'm on the morning shift tomorrow.'

Tom drained his drink. 'I'll take you,' he said and they began their escape through the garden.

'I should say goodbye,' she stopped abruptly.

'No, they'll understand. We'll never get away otherwise.' He took her hand and steered her towards the driveway.

He drove slowly, aware that he was slightly drunk and the roads, unblessed by streetlights, were dark and narrow with a steep precipice on one side.

'Did you have a good time?' he asked.

'Yeah.' She had curled up, her head laid back against the seat. 'I see them coming and going at the airport so it's interesting to see them in another setting. They seem very much at home here.'

Was there a trace of irony in her voice? He wasn't sure.

'Be careful,' he said, 'there are some dangerous sharks there.'

She grinned sleepily. 'Don't worry, I know I'm tonight's bit of local colour.'

He parked outside her house and she kissed him lightly on the cheek. 'Thanks,' she said. 'See you.' She let herself quietly into her house.

Back in his villa he wondered if she had included him in that general dismissal . . . 'tonight's bit of local colour'. He saw himself palely in the plate glass window, tall, handsome, forty, 'and white', he added. 'Predatory,' the word nosed unpleasantly into his consciousness, swam there through the rum fumes like a pale, ugly shark. He thought suddenly of his wife, skis flying, dark against the white snow and the scream and the arc of tossed snow and the crumple of her against the dark tree and the terrible guilt later for, even in his grieving, he knew that he no longer loved her, had not loved her for a long time, not like those early nights, the long talks and mornings, her head a golden crown on the pillow. It was only since coming here, to this quiet, uncluttered house, that he had felt again that early love, the rushing back to say things that had not been said, the reaching forward for things not yet ready for words and the absolute belief that they were magical, not vulnerable to any sort of destruction. So that when they had come, in such small steps, the tiny, brittle silences, the little criticisms, he had not noticed but ridiculously it was the room he had first noticed, hung about with the trappings of a life he did not want.

Peter lay in bed, arms crossed behind his head, staring out past a scraggly garden to the crowded street. A thin boy in ragged clothes hurled his pushcart in between a car and a bus, narrowly missing a collision between all three. The bus driver hurled a stream of invective at him. The man in the car mopped his brow nervously and the boy sped away laughing. Three men sat outside a bar noisily playing dominoes occasionally aiming a kick at a couple of mangy dogs who were sniffing around in the gutter for non-existent scraps. A woman with a large, pregnant belly was embroiled in a heated argument with a man, he punched her in the face and a few passers-by paused, drew closer, watching with a cold curiosity to see the outcome of the fight.

Everything about the scene filled Peter with revulsion and he turned his head away, hungrily seeking his mother's eyes, her face smiling cheerfully out at him from a framed photograph.

Blonde hair curled about her face and she held a picture hat, trimmed with ribbons which fluttered against her raised arm. His father, dark and correct, stood slightly behind her, almost out of the frame. Beside them was a photo of himself and Evan as children, the crossed genetic mirror of these parents. Evan, dark like his father, holding himself almost out of the picture, his face a boyish replica of his mother's delicate English features. Peter, laughing in the centre, blonde, curly hair framing his father's rugged, negro features which had been copied in a paler brush stroke.

Peter stared at the photos until Evan and his father melted at the edges and they were together; carefree, beautiful, rich, they stood on a wide verandah looking out across the vast acres of an Argentine ranch. She raised her hand and the ribbons on her hat fluttered against his face.

'All yours, of course darling,' she said.

They walked down the steps, her arm in his, to meet the chauffeur who had brought a shiny, red Ferrari up the driveway and parked it beside them.

'Like it darling? Thought it might be fun for you.'

He kissed her on both cheeks and held out his hand for the key which the chauffeur dropped into his open palm.

It was always like that, far away from the impoverished streets of this miserable country town. Away from Evan nagging him about getting a job.

'But I have a job. Lord and Lady Smalling, you know. I'm their on-site manager, you know, property, business, all that, you know.'

Evan did know. He knew only too well that Peter had no job, no salary. He hated seeing him, so lacking in direction, content to be a hanger-on in other people's lives.

'You've got to make your own way in life,' he told Peter. 'You can join me in the business, it's doing well now and I could do with some help.'

But that would start other arguments and in the small house, the gulf between the brothers grew. Evan left the anxieties about his brother for the comfort of a catalogue full of new power tools with ingenious attachments. But his mind wandered. He had a sudden image of himself, a teenager working in Brown's hardware store after his Dad died, clutching his first week's pay, such a small amount, but it would go towards Peter's school fees. Another very similar image, standing at home, clutching the note his mother had left, the mix of apprehension, how to tell Peter when he came in from school, the guilty relief that she had gone. He did not earn enough to support her, so beautiful, so charming, so impractical. He turned a page of the catalogue. Wherever she was he hoped she was happy and being taken care of, for he had a nagging picture of her, ageing, alone at the bar of some seedy South American hotel.

Peter had no intention of grubbing around in a dusty old hardware store on the busy main street, so he set out to make himself indispensable to the Smallings, particularly to Claire Smalling. Although he was only in his early twenties he carefully developed a mature, nonchalant style. He would seduce her. She would be so grateful, so happy to have a young, attractive lover that she would shower him with gifts and leave her rather dashing little MG with him when she returned, disconsolate, to London.

Claire chatted endlessly to him and used him as her unpaid chauffeur, particularly for her assignations with a tall, gangly German whose wife appeared to be both blind and deaf to the torrid affair that was taking place in her home. Peter was fascinated with Claire, her cornflower blue eyes, her tanned, energetic body. He enjoyed her stories of dangerous sexual escapades and her ability to do exactly as she pleased thrilled him. He drank in the names of famous people in famous places and became a devoted Anglophile, developing a clear and resonant British accent and a penchant for wearing silk cravats tucked neatly into his crisp, cotton shirts. He was, however, becoming frustrated with Claire's refusal to see him as a desirable replacement for the German marionette.

'I used to mess around with boys,' she laughed at him once when he suggested that she consider a younger lover. 'Trouble was, I had to spend so much time turning them into decent lovers. By the time I got them into shape they turned clinging and I became bored with them.'

Henry never seemed to go out. He read the English newspapers which were couriered in for him, conducted business on the telephone and swam in the pool in the garden. One day, Peter went to take Claire for an appointment only to find that the car had gone in for servicing and she had gone off with a woman friend. In response to a languid wave, he joined Henry for a drink in the lattice enclosed pool cabana. Henry was interested in Peter's plans for the future so Peter told him that he was going into real estate and property development. Henry thought it a 'capital' idea and encouraged Peter to read the real estate sections of his English newspapers. On the days while he waited for Claire, he would drive around compiling information on vacant lots, on ownership of certain large houses, on a suitable office in a new building which was soaring up above the narrow winding streets and dilapidated houses.

Evan was happy to see Peter focused on something and listened intently to his plans for a new business. However, with the recent expansion of his hardware store, his cash was rather 'tied up' at the moment.

'But you could start right here,' he said. 'We could easily convert the living room into an office, maybe start with rentals. When the cash flow starts picking up, we could buy a house, fix it up and sell it. Do you know,' he warmed to the topic, 'everybody is building for the tourists who are here today, gone tomorrow. Nobody is bothering about where we Jamaicans are going to live. Just look at all the banks and businesses opening up here and the hotels taking on out-of-town staff. All those accountants and secretaries and bank clerks are going to need places to live. Man, this town has got to grow!'

Peter fell silent. Why the hell did Evan always have to do things the hard way? He was depressed by his brother's lack of vision. Big houses for the tourists were the thing, profits in foreign exchange which would not be devalued, swimming pools and lush gardens, not, for God's sake, reclaiming tacky little houses for bank clerks and secretaries.

*

In Chicago, a handful of zealous animal lovers were attracting a great deal of media attention with some unpleasantly clear and detailed photographs, taken at the Endelbaum mink ranch, of the little creatures being killed and skinned. Lester departed abruptly for Chicago leaving Rose who soon replaced Peter as Claire's escort for long afternoon jaunts. Peter was not unduly saddened by this sudden turn of events. He was engrossed in his new project and welcomed the opportunity to chat with Henry about the fine points of property development. The friendship was developing well and with liberal amounts of gin and tonic, cool and frosty in heavy crystal glasses, the 'my dear chap's' were becoming warmer and more frequent. Happily, Henry never once asked him about the nature of his 'job' with Claire or why he had been jettisoned in favour of Rose with the fine, dark eyes and the hoarse American voice.

Warmed by the comradely, accepting nature of the friendship, Peter decided to approach Henry to invest in his 'Global Property Development', Managing Director, Peter Johnston. They were ensconced in Henry's study, sipping gin and tonic and gazing out through the open french windows at the garden stretching out, flawlessly green. However, before Peter could get the conversation properly started, Henry began one of his own. He moved over to close the shutters.

'Bit of a glare today, wouldn't you say.'

He sat down beside Peter on a couch covered in pale grey velvet and took his hand in his. His long, sheepdog face had acquired an attractive, golden tan and Peter noticed that there were little flecks of grey in his hair. Henry told Peter that he had grown very fond of him and very concerned about his future in a backwoods like Jamaica where his talents and good looks were obviously not appreciated. With a charming and practised shyness he proceeded to seduce Peter.

Tom rolled another sheet of paper into the typewriter. After many false starts he began to concentrate, to shut out everything else but the words flying like ski tracks on the white paper. The house closed in gently around him. Mae polishing the furniture, her husband Sebert out in the garden pruning and clipping. When he lifted his eyes from the page he saw a riot of colours in the garden, an endlessly blue sky. Wrapped in warmth, everything soft at the edges, he at last found it possible to write of the cold, the harried pace that had caught him and kept him blind to the changes moving steadily into the pattern of their lives. So much that had seemed important now spread itself on the page, dissected, revealed for the hollow creature that it was. Yet, in the flying white pages he wondered if he was betraying her, pulling away the covers from her sleeping head, or if it was an act of cowardly self-preservation and he was in fact pulling the sheet up over that golden pillowed head.

On a rare trip into town, hunting for typewriter ribbons, he saw Claudia. They fell into an easy conversation and ended up having lunch together. He told her that he was writing again.

'Oh, so that's why I haven't seen you at Claire's,' she said.

He felt a small tremor of fear. 'Yeah, I've been kinda busy, but also I didn't want to get too involved with them.'

'They're OK.' As if sensing his concern, she smiled reassuringly at him.

'I haven't been that often myself, but Claire has been encouraging me to go to London with them. She seems to think she can turn me into a model.' She laughed, a curious mixture of defiance and mockery. 'Can't imagine me being a model, but it would be nice to travel. It's funny that I work at the airport but have never been on a plane myself.'

Tom frowned and signalled the waiter for another round of drinks.

'I know,' she continued, 'I'm this winter's fad. The pretty, little black girl. But what's the worst that could happen if I went? They would get tired of me or me of them and I'd come home.'

'Don't go,' he said abruptly. 'They're too sophisticated for you. I was once mixed up with some people who were rather like them, fascinated with beauty, with novelty. It's very dangerous.'

'I can take care of myself,' she said sharply, 'I'm not stupid you know.'

86

She closed her knife and fork with a sudden, irritable gesture and he noticed that her hands were small, schoolgirl hands with the nails bitten off. They looked vulnerable, lying there, slightly clenched against the white tablecloth.

'What's it matter to you anyway?' She sounded tired, dispirited. 'I guess you would like to see me forever as some kind of sweet, little island girl. You survived the big city and you're doing fine. Why shouldn't I?'

'I almost didn't survive,' he said softly, touching her fingertips.

She looked at him in silence for a while and turned her palm up, lacing her fingers lightly in his.

'I'm sorry,' she said. 'I guess I don't really know much about you.'

'That makes two of us,' he said and they laughed.

It was raining when he got back to the villa, a light, silvery rain, filtering the sun into a hazy screen, soft fingertips pressing at the windowpane. He wanted desperately to see her, to have her come to the villa, sit with him at the round, polished mahogany table reflecting the fluted shapes of hibiscus which Mae arranged fresh each day. He wanted her to hear the quiet of night except for the tree frogs chirping outside his window. He wanted her in his bed. 'And then what?' he thought. 'I'd be no better than the Smallings.' Intent on seduction, wanting to possess that innocence, that poise, that sense of herself and her relatedness to this place.

He wandered restlessly from window to window. There was an unpleasant sensation in the pit of his stomach and he poured himself a drink. Standing there, looking at the amber of the rum against the cold hardness of the ice cubes he realized that he was worse. At least they were offering a trip to London, he was offering nothing at all. His publisher was urging him to return to New York, he could not take her there. He felt heavy, old, he would become immensely watchful, hovering over her until she panicked from the enclosure of it. And if he did not . . . if he allowed her to find her own way in the city. He felt an unbearable sadness as if she had been very close to him but was moving, noiselessly away, like a boat slipped from its moorings, drifting down a dark, heavy river.

Peter was waking up in the mornings hungover and filled with panic. Henry would not make any commitment to 'Global Property Development'. He was not even inviting him to come to London although he and Claire were all over Claudia with nonsense about making her into a model. He was alternatively terrified by and fascinated with Henry. He could not stay away but when he was there he feared that Henry would abandon him, that Claire would find out, that worse, the servants would find out and fill the town with their gossip. He knew only too well how Evan and his friends would react. He knew how they expressed themselves on that subject, the utter scorn, derision, anger he would face. He had started having blinding headaches which held him prisoner in his room with all the light shut out but he could not shut out the strange, disjointed images that pressed in on him. His mother, her arm severed, floating above her head, waving a hat with dark, red ribbons. His father clutching his chest while the child Peter stood rooted to the floor gasping, unable to call for help. Henry's long, doggy face smiling tenderly at him.

He would put an end to it. He would talk to Henry, either he would go to London with them or Henry would set him up in business here. Peter dressed carefully, borrowed Evan's battered old Escort and drove up to the Smallings. The house was full of people.

'My dear chap,' said Henry, as Peter opened the discussion, 'I promise we shall talk about it very, very soon. Just as soon as we have a moment to ourselves. Now run along and fetch us some drinks won't you. There's a dear boy.' And his face bent close to Peter's was suffused with charm and affection.

Dinner was an interminable affair. Claire's voice clipped insistently into the fabric of the conversation until it lay shredded over the melting tangerine sherbert and the neat, pale, accompanying vanilla wafers. Peter felt hot and nausea rolled up into the back of his throat although he had eaten nothing. He left, got the old car into a halting splutter and set off. It was raining and he drove slowly, peering into the faint beam of the headlights for the outline of the dark road. His head was throbbing. It felt as if someone was pushing a knife into his temples, withdrawing it and pushing it in, over and over again. Suddenly tears gushed from his eyes and the pain lessened slightly before it turned once more and plunged straight through his skull.

The Smallings departed for London having debated whether or not they should send a wreath. They decided against it. Tom heard about the accident on the radio right after an announcement that the tourist season was nearly over and Jamaicans were to be nice to the tourists so that they would want to 'make it Jamaica again'. Tom felt a flash of pity for the boy, so young, only twenty-two. He was probably speeding. Jamaicans were such damned crazy drivers. He returned his attention to the typewriter. His publisher was now insistent on his return and he had exhausted his advance.

Claudia also heard it on the radio. She felt very sad about it, he was the same age as her even though he had seemed older when they met occasionally at the Smallings. As she walked up the road to get the bus for the airport, she noticed that a new family had moved into the teacher's old house. She wondered what had happened to the teacher's wife and their bright, attractive children.

In the Hills

Up in these hills the mornings bloom so gently moist, everything so wet with dew and wrapped in pale grey that you want desperately to hold your arms out, to pull it all to you and hold it there for an hour, keep it with you for a space of time. But the sun, busy auntie, rushes out and tidies it all away so quickly you can hardly believe your grey moment was ever there. Later, the busy, rushing sun will spread herself out and reign expansively throughout the hills.

Years before, I had left the heat and the noise and the warring of the city to build my small house here on my mother's land. The land had been new and difficult to work, but now it was yielding up its crops regularly and I had become part of the cycle of planting and weeding and watering and reaping. My nearest neighbour was some few chains away down the hill. A silent old man who kept a few cows and walked the two miles to the village to sell his milk. On Saturday he stayed in the village to get his drinking evening in and on very clear Saturday nights I could hear him singing his way home with unctuous, richly turned psalms.

A few miles further up the mountain lay a forest reserve. Land carefully planted out with firs. I became aware, gradually, that something was going on up there. A coming and a going and sudden noises of jeeps rumbling up and down the stony road. The first time I saw them they were clearly city youths. Tight trousers and skinny T-shirts, hair luxuriously uncombed and lazy, slouchy hips and talking, so much talking all the time. A week later I saw them drilling, soft cat manoeuvres, boys' games played with stony eyes.

Twice a week the big shots came to talk, to stir the blood, to lay strong reasons why they should learn the war game and be prepared to play it out down in the dusty city. These leaders walked like men but their repeated jargon sounded like gun fire under the firs and in silence I watched the scene close up like the stilted figures in a Noh play.

One of the boys came to my house. He wanted vegetables for the group. I let him have them, making myself sound simpler and more crazy than in the days when I was really ill. Soon they became greedy, they wanted the corn and beans before they were even full. I told them there would be more for all if they waited but they said their time was now and they could not wait. One Saturday afternoon a boy came on his own. He asked for nothing but stood silently near my front step and looked around. I took no notice of him but busied myself with my tomato plants, pinching out the first buds so the plant would not bear until it was strong enough. The sun was going down and still he stood there, his dark eyes large and quiet in his thin face. I went inside and made a quick supper for us, bread and plantain and fresh carrot juice to wash it down. We sat on my verandah until eventually I asked him,

'What is it, are you afraid?'

His thin body moved suddenly, jerkily and he looked at me.

'Yes,' he said. 'I can see no way out.'

He spoke for a while then of his hot, bitter existence in the city. No job, no money for him. When the big ones spoke it had sounded so simple. Stay with me, learn to hate, learn to kill and you will have a job, you will have a house and you will be free. Free from the oppressors.

He sat there as the evening turned into night, and he said, 'I am afraid to kill another man. It is a sin to kill. And afterwards, what job can I get that will make me forget what I have done? What pride can I take in my house if I have such a sin in my heart?'

I had no answer of course, I could only watch the lines of his thin body aching with pain as he sat there on my small verandah.

91

'What do the big shots tell you,' I asked. 'How do they make it seem all right to the others?'

He sighed and I saw the shine of tears in his eyes.

'They say,' he whispered, 'that we are all oppressed, that we cannot all be free to enjoy the new society unless all make the sacrifices. They say we will be heroes and our names will be written in the history books.'

I looked out into the starry sky and heard my old neighbour singing his way home up the hill.

'So, that is a good thing,' I said. 'If none of you have anything now you will all have to do something together to get what you want.'

The boy looked at his hands and then folded them round his body. He suddenly seemed very young indeed.

'Perhaps there is another way,' he said. 'This way, they will get what they want. They will always have us then because we shall have to live with what they have made us create.'

I shivered then, on my small verandah, and went inside to fetch a shawl. I suggested we make some hot tea and he came inside and helped me light the lamp. The dirty things from supper still lay on the table in the alcove that I call my kitchen. He fetched some water from the big oil drum out back and washed our few things while I waited for the kettle to boil. He was quick and economical with his movements in the small space which only I had moved in for so many years.

We took our tea back out to the verandah and found to our delight that the moon, which had been struggling up over the hill, had made it to the top and lay flatly gleaming into our verandah. For the first time he smiled and threw back his head to catch the gleam of the light under his half-closed eyelids. But he grew serious again and blew on his tea to cool it.

'You could leave,' I said, testing him. 'Run away.'

'No,' he said firmly. 'I am in the group now and there is no way out. There was no way out when I was in the city and there will never be a way out for me now.'

The warm tea eased its way past the back of my closed throat. I said, 'I used to live in the city. I had access to money, on

92

terms. I too was in a box, a prison. It took me a long time to find my way out, but I did. You will find your way out in your own time.'

He set the cup down and looked carefully at me.

'I used to think that way once,' he said. And then he was walking down the step and out across my garden and off into the hills.

Up in these hills the mornings are so soft and moist that you want, just for one moment, to gather it all to you. To hold, just for that second a soft, new life before that overriding sun burns and dries it flat away.

Mint Tea

The dress was pink, a very fashionable sort of dusty rose, like fading petals, and Mother had lent her her pearl ear-rings. She could see them gleaming softly when she turned her head and peered into the dim reflection of the mirror. Late afternoon sun fell through the jalousie windows and left gold bars on the wooden floor. Annie hurried in then stepped slowly over them, her shiny patent pumps made her feet look very small, very neat. They stood together, the sisters, looking into the mirror and they smiled slightly into each other's eyes. Florence moved to the door and looked out past the verandah where Father was standing with the horse and buggy, and she caught her breath slightly at the sight of them. Father, so tall and handsome in his dark suit, the brown gleam of the horse and beyond them the mountains. A bird was singing somewhere and Father bent, picked a rose and placed it carefully in his lapel. That bush by the front steps, how it bloomed, always covered in small, fragrant red roses.

The Town Hall had been decorated with palm fronds and hibiscus flowers and they sat in the front row, very important, very grown up. One of the singers, a tall, thin fair man with a moustache, sang all the love songs to Annie and Florence saw Annie's dark, almond-shaped eyes, turned up to him under the perfect wings of her eyebrows. Afterwards, Father bustled them away before 'that city man' could make their acquaintance, hurried them into the buggy and they drove off, up the hilly road. So many bright stars and she and Annie sang one of the songs:

> 'I'll remember you, always
> with a love that's true, always.'

Florence shook her head slightly, as if to dust off the fine powder of memories that seemed increasingly to settle around her mind. It was all so long ago, she thought, yet often her childhood seemed more real, more vivid than this pale, creased up thing that was retirement. Each day so similar, each day so quiet without the regular sound of the school bell signalling a gush of noise as the children streamed out of class.

There was a knock at the gate. Startled, Florence looked out and saw a young woman standing there.

'Please mam, I looking a job as a live-in helper.'

It was mid-afternoon and very hot. The girl looked weary and her dress had dark, wet stains spreading out from her armpits.

'I don't need anyone,' said Florence.

'Please mam,' the girl called quickly. 'I could have a drink of water?'

Florence got her some water and motioned for her to push the gate and come in. The girl came in and stood by the front steps holding a small, brown, vinyl bag. The sun was so hot she began to feel confused and when Florence gave her the water, she drank it too quickly and felt slightly sick so that she leaned for a moment against the verandah wall.

'Child, are you ill?'

'No mam. I been walking since morning looking a job.'

'Come, sit on the verandah for a while.'

Esmie walked up the two steps to the verandah and sat on a wooden slatted chair.

'Where are you from?'

'I name Esmie Grant and I grow at Haven Home and I am eighteen years of age.'

Florence gazed at the girl, an awkward, bony sort of body and a face without expression. Her hair was plaited neatly in two sections, a schoolgirl hairstyle, but there was something old, tired looking about her eyes.

'Well,' said Florence firmly, 'you must go back to the Home now, it will soon be dark.'

'I can't go back mam. I am eighteen and I have to leave.'

'You left the Home with no job and no place to go?'

'I don't have no family mam. I have to get a job.'

'What kind of work can you do Esmie?'

'Well mam, my head wasn't so good wid de books but I used to mind de smaller children.'

Florence felt a wave of anger, how could the Home just put her out, no arrangements made for her at all. No wonder so many of these girls ended up on the streets.

'Have you eaten anything since morning?'

'No mam.'

Florence fixed some sandwiches and lemonade, gave them to Esmie and then went inside to call the Home. The Matron confirmed that she had left there that day, that she was a decent girl but had no special skills.

'But how on earth,' Florence asked angrily,' can you put the girl out and she knows no one, has no place to go.'

'Rules are rules,' Matron replied huffily. The place was already overcrowded, every day there were little ones coming in, and they didn't have staff enough as it was to look after the babies. There was no one to be out finding jobs for the big girls. They would just have to get out there and stand on their own two feet.

Florence brought the conversation to a close and hung up. She hated volubility and she hated complainers and Matron was afflicted with both ailments. Florence returned to the verandah and looked at Esmie.

'Esmie, my name is Miss Gates. I am a retired teacher and I do not have a job for you, but I have a little room at the back and you can stay there for a day or two while you look for a job. But remember that it's only for a short time. The Lord helps those that help themselves so you must do your best to find a job.'

'Yes mam. Thank you mam.' Esmie smiled shyly and Florence saw that her face, rescued briefly by the smile, was pretty.

'And I'm telling you straight,' Florence added, 'keep your

mind on sensible things, don't let me see you getting in with any foolish boys.'

Esmie shook her head wearily.

Florence set her to clean out the little room which hadn't been used for years. There was a bed, an old dressing table and the naked light bulb illuminated unkindly the drabness of it. But Florence fetched some curtains, an old blue bedspread and a lace-edged doily for the dressing table so that it looked quite habitable when they were finished. As Esmie unpacked her bag, Florence turned away saddened by the sight.Two dresses, two sets of underwear and a tin of lavender talc. Florence added some toilet articles and a Bible and so Esmie was set up in a corner of Miss Gates' life.

Esmie was neat, tidy, dutiful but she had no skills for job-hunting. Florence was horrified to discover that she could barely read and write and she would only respond to direct questions. 'An underdeveloped soul,' she thought sadly and set herself diligently to Esmie's instruction. But in spite of Florence's considerable experience as a teacher, Esmie proved an unrespon-sive pupil. Florence encouraged her to read the newspaper and listen to the radio but Esmie seemed to have no real interest in any particular subject, she had no particular liking for one thing or dislike for another. She did as she was told. 'Institution life,' thought Florence and she tried to get her to make simple decisions. Should they have chicken or beef for dinner, eggs or porridge for breakfast.

The weeks passed. Since her retirement, since so many of her friends had long since died, Florence had a dread of becoming a lonely, muddled old woman. She established a very stable routine for herself, one that kept mind and body active. She kept her house tidy, she gardened, she read and she went to church on Sunday. But recently, she had found herself sitting somewhere, perhaps with some mending on her lap, caught up in vivid memories of the past. The early morning smell of the mountains mixed with the light and birds singing. They came over her in a wave, so fresh that she would tilt her face up absorbing the smell of moist leaves and opening flowers and then the sound of

Mother in the kitchen grinding coffee beans and she would wait for that smell to form itself, to come slipping out to make the signal that woke up the rest of the house. Mother and Father, Annie, beautiful Annie. They were all dead now and sometimes she felt that she had lived too long and it was time that she too moved on to another life. But here she was with a stranger for company.

Sometimes she grew irritated with Esmie, she was never going to find a job and move on and she didn't want the responsibility of this girl who seemed to progress so very slowly. At other times she was overwhelmed with pity for her, never having had her own parents, her own home.

One Sunday she persuaded Esmie to go to church with her. Esmie sat quiet until the first hymn and then she opened her mouth and a voice so beautiful poured out that Florence found her own strong contralto dropping to a whisper to listen to the effortless, golden soprano pouring out beside her. Esmie's eyes were half-closed, her face expressionless, the voice just rose and streamed out of her body and Esmie seemed quite unaware of it.

After church Florence suggested that she should join the choir.

'No mam,' said Esmie.

Florence was stunned.

'But Esmie, you have been blessed with a beautiful voice, it's a God-given talent. You should join the choir and develop your voice.'

Esmie looked away. She was disinterested in the conversation, unmoved by the compliment.

'I going to change my frock mam and start the dinner.' Esmie said, moving away quickly.

'For heaven's sake Esmie, stop calling me "mam".' Florence said wearily.

The next day, Florence sent for the piano tuner. He spent hours with his tuning forks and his notes played over and over again. Esmie gave him tea and ignored him but the noise made Florence irritable, she went out for a walk and found herself looking at things in shops. It seemed to her that the shops were full of ugly, badly made things from places like Taiwan and

Hong Kong. She decided to buy Esmie a dress but the prices were way above the few notes tucked into her handbag. She returned home hot, tired and bad-tempered. The piano tuner charged an exorbitant fee for his services and left. She drew the curtains in her bedroom and lay down. She was hot, her feet were swollen and her thoughts raced about, disjointed. Her heart was beating too quickly, she must calm herself, breathe in slowly, out slowly . . .

It was growing dark and Esmie did not know what to fix for supper. Miss Gates never lay down like that, in the day. She went to the bedroom door.

'You sick mam, Miss Gates?' she asked. 'You want I should fix you some mint tea?'

'Yes thank you Esmie,' she said, pleased that Esmie had taken the initiative in this one, small act.

Revived by the tea, she found a box of old music sheets and began haltingly at first, then the notes seemed to flow back into her fingers, and she gathered up confidence and launched out fully. Esmie sat on the verandah waiting patiently for Miss Gates to stop playing and tell her what to fix for supper. But Miss Gates flowed on and finally Esmie fixed herself a sandwich and went to her room. She was later summoned and when she went, sleepily to the living room she was startled by the old lady's face, the excitement there, her eyes sparkled and her close cropped white hair seemed to crackle around her head. She gave her some sheets of music.

'It's the twenty-third Psalm, you know the words already. I'm going to play the music and you listen and follow the words on the song sheet.'

Esmie took the paper and listened as Miss Gates played and sang in her slightly raspy old contralto voice.

'Now ready? I'm going to start again and you sing it with me.'

Miss Gates played and Esmie sang. She grasped the music immediately and once more the effortless, true voice flowed out.

When it was finished Miss Gates looked at her, still with that sparkle and energy about her.

'Wonderful Esmie. Just truly wonderful. We will practise a few more times and then you will sing in church in Sunday.'

'No mam,' said Esmie.

99

Miss Gates flew into a terrible temper. 'Don't you dare tell me "no". So foolish. Why ever not? I can't understand you at all.'

Esmie said nothing but she began to feel a bit anxious, she did not want Miss Gates to get upset. She did not want her to get sick. Miss Gates closed the piano lid and paced up and down in front of the immobile Esmie.

'I have been a teacher all my life. Some were bright, some were not, but they all left my class with something, some sense of themselves, some spark of ambition. Are you listening? I pick up the newspaper every day and see this one or that one, doing well, doing something with their lives. And you, with this great, natural talent, you have no ambition. For the life of me I can't understand it.'

'Please Miss Gates,' Esmie said softly, 'please dont tek on so.'

Florence stopped pacing. She felt dreadfully tired. They locked up the house and went to their rooms. The next day she spent most of the day in her room and she would not eat. Esmie did not know what to do. She knew there was a niece who talked on the telephone sometimes with Miss Gates, but Esmie did not know her name or phone number. If anything happened to the old lady she would not know what to do.

The next day Miss Gates did not even get dressed. She accepted a cup of tea and stayed in bed. There was no washing to do, the house was tidy and Esmie did not know what to do. She knew she must do something. Finally she presented herself at the door.

'Miss Gates, mam.'

'Yes Esmie?'

Esmie was shocked by the voice, by the face that turned towards her. She looked so old, so small and old.

'Mam, I should get a doctor? What I should do mam?'

Miss Gates turned her head away and did not reply.

Esmie went away. She was frightened now, she was trembling and she felt cold. It was always hot in the Home. There were so many girls. Sometimes she would wake up at night and feel glad that she was awake in the cool and quiet of the night. She went to her room and picked up the Bible Miss Gates had given her.

She held it in her hands, not reading it, just feeling the soft, worn leather cover and the slight weight of it in her hands. She liked having her own room there. Miss Gates put up white net curtains and she liked to wake up in the mornings and see them moving slightly, they looked so light as if they were not quite real. Juliet was her friend at the Home but when Juliet was fourteen a lady came from England and said that she was Juliet's aunt, she cried, standing there by Juliet's bed. She had a big bosom and she cried and her bosom heaved up and down. She took Juliet away to live with her. Esmie thought of Miss Gates lying in her room looking so sad and old, she did not want her to go away like Juliet. Then she remembered that she had been pleased when she gave her mint tea. She would make her some tea. She quickly picked some mint and hurried to the kitchen. The mint tea would make the old lady feel better and things would be as they were before. She did not want things to change. She was cold and trembling, she must make the tea quickly, it would make the old lady well again. She reached for a cup and it fell, smashed to bits on the floor. She fell to the floor, picked up a piece of the cup and started to weep.

Florence heard the noise and then silence.

'Esmie, what's that?' There was no reply.

She got up slowly, wearily pulled on a dressing gown and made her way to the kitchen. Esmie was sitting on the floor, blood dripped from her hand, very dark against the pale tiles of the kitchen floor.

'But child, what's wrong? Get up and let me have a look at that hand.'

Esmie sat, crumpled up. She made no sound but tears streamed from her eyes which were wide open, staring.

'Esmie, get up this minute. Get off that floor.'

Esmie stared straight ahead of her.

'Mama, mama,' her voice was that of a very small child. Then the voice became adult, a soft, crooning voice.

'Mama soon come back baby. I going to church. I going to sing a lovely song for my baby. See your Daddy come to stay wid you. I soon come back.'

Esmie stopped crying, her eyes stared straight in front of her, she was absolutely still, in shock.

Florence stood, leaning against the kitchen counter, her breathing uneven, loud in the still room. Finally she helped Esmie up, bandaged her hand and put her to lie on the sofa.

'What happened Esmie? What happened to your Mama?'

Esmie's voice was flat and toneless. 'De house catch on fire. Me Daddy give me to somebody an tried was to put out de fire. Mama was coming back from church and she see, she run to save me but she an him dead in de fire. I don't know why dem never leave me in dere too. I don't know why.'

'Esmie, how old were you when that happened?'

'I was very small. I never realize it before. I used to have bad dreams.' For a moment she looked hopefully at Miss Gates. 'Maybe is me mixing up de dreams.'

They sat in silence for a long while. The afternoon sun fell through the window in a bright, slatted pattern. It reminded Florence of something. She must remember. Yes, the afternoon that they went to the concert. How excited they were, how grown-up to be going out with Father and how the city man stared and sang love songs to Annie. The next year, she went away to teacher's college and Annie ran away with an American who was studying something in the hills. He was a geologist, that was it. He was an atheist, he did not believe in marriage and Father was set against the friendship, besides he was a big, grown man and Annie was only seventeen. But after that everything was troubled and her memories stopped there. There were earlier ones, of them wading in the river, of Mother teaching them to sing and play the piano, of Father setting off for work, so neat and correct, to run the Farmers' Credit Union in the nearby town. But somehow, after that evening at the concert she found she had to choose her memories more carefully. Her adult life had been full, busy, yet she had screened them out, too many were better left unexamined. Esmie stirred on the sofa and a cushion fell to the floor. Florence picked it up and settled it behind her head.

The light changed and Florence went out on the verandah to

see the last of the sunset. A bird was singing and she looked around slowly, searching through the small garden, but it was hidden somewhere and she couldn't see it. Only the sound came, pure, unhesitant as the afternoon faded and the evening asserted itself darkly around her.

Nellie

She had found it all very interesting at first. Now she was cold, the airconditioning was up too high and she longed to be out in the fresh air. This year, the expressions were, 'ensuring access', 'equitability of resources', 'sustainable development'. She listened to them rolling off so easily, in a variety of accents, a sort of verbal talisman against defeat. She also knew the reality, the small, ill-equipped clinics with rows of mothers queuing up for immunization shots for their babies, or for family planning methods, or for a multitude of ailments, for which there were not enough medicines.

She tried to concentrate on the presentation from Trinidad. An attractive man with a long title was speaking and she listened with only half an ear to the content while she enjoyed the lilt of his accent. Horace had decided to go to Carnival in Trinidad this year and she had been amused at the contortions he had gotten into because he did not want her to go with him.

She had made it easy for him.

'What a pity that I can't go,' she said. 'You know I have this conference coming up in Washington.'

And so it had been settled and he had gone with a show of reluctance, he was only going really because the 'boys' were going.

She adjusted her conference papers, although they were already impeccably arranged, and noted, with a small frown of annoyance, that she had snagged one of her neatly filed, unpolished nails.

It was over. They could leave. There would be a reception

104

later that evening and then three more days of talks. 'I can't bear it,' she thought, steering her way out to the foyer and on to the small bus waiting to take them back to their hotel. A young man got on and sat beside her.

'I enjoyed your presentation this morning. You struck just the right note of pride and mendicancy.'

'Oh Lord,' she smiled, 'don't let anyone hear you say that. We're all trying so hard to pretend that we're not desperate, that we don't resent having to "perform" for the damn aid because we know full well that we daren't go home without at least a significant promise.'

His name tag identified him as Dr Sam Bowen and he was also Jamaican. 'What's your interest in all this?' she asked.

'I'm applying for a job with . . .' and he named one of the large international health agencies. 'So I thought I should seem knowledgeable about what was going on in the region.'

She felt a tinge of annoyance, yet another professional deserting, chasing after the big money, then immediately felt that she was probably being unfair, judgemental. They talked for a while and she found out that he was in research and he was, in fact, being recruited to work on a parasitology project which involved several other countries.

'That should be interesting,' she said, hoping that he was not going to bore her with details of tapeworms.

He did not and they parted amicably at the hotel.

Nellie took a long, hot bath and reluctantly prepared for the reception. She felt restless, irritable. She combed her hair and saw a clump of grey hairs curling delicately at her temples. They looked very white against her brown skin and she wondered if she should pull them out. She examined her face closely, a few wrinkles at the corners of her eyes, and those sparkling, robust grey hairs.

'What do I want,' she wondered, 'what the hell do I want?'

She lay on her bed for a while, staring at the bland hotel furnishings and the ubiquitous Gideon Bible. So many hotel rooms, in all sorts of places. So many conferences and seminars, she was weary of it all. She was also weary of Horace. About a year ago she had suddenly stopped caring about his affairs. They no longer bothered her. She felt even sorry for the women, so ill at ease, and only able to be relaxed with her when it was over. She would never have any women friends at this rate.

It was all so silly, so pointless, this endless chasing and mating. He wouldn't talk about it, of course, as the pretence was that they were such a happy, successful couple. And indeed they were. Letters came addressed to them as Mr and Mrs. They had dinner parties, they agreed about politics and supported the same charities. Horace had his affairs and sometimes she thought he had them just to keep in with the swing of things, it was expected of an attractive, successful man. For he had made it plain, after a stormy evening of accusations on her part, denials on his, that he had no intention of leaving. He was happy in his marriage. But she knew, he loved the thrill of flirtation, he liked variety and conquest and Horace liked women physically. He was a connoisseur of breasts and legs and he always chose intelligent, independent women who would not become clinging or demanding as Horace was also a bit mean. He did not want to have to get into taking this one out to expensive dinners or into buying that one costly little trinkets. He was horrified by those of his friends who had dependent, young girlfriends who needed to have the rent paid, the trip to Miami paid for and threw tantrums if the birthday gift was not sparkling enough. No, Horace did not want the expense nor the possibility of unpleasant scenes. He valued privacy and discretion. Having an attractive and intelligent wife and having affairs with bright, emancipated women was a perfect situation.

'Why stay?' she wondered. The situation was comfortable for her also. She liked her work, she liked the large, attractive home that they had made together. She did not want to be out there, a woman alone, she liked being part of a family, part of so many little routines, observances. And besides, she had a sort of horror at the thought of being seen as being alone, in need of masculine attention. She shuddered at the thought of being with another man in an intimate situation, taking off her clothes, revealing herself to someone she didn't really know. It was not a suitable situation for her, that was all, even the word 'boyfriend' sounded ridiculous.

She got up and finished dressing. 'Maybe I'm not really unhappy at all,' she thought. 'I just think I should be because my husband chooses to be unfaithful.' And she laughed at herself because it was really very foolish to choose to be unhappy over the choices and behaviour of someone else.

People milled around in the reception room and ate strange things on little pieces of toast. Sam turned up and offered to fetch her a drink and they stood talking for a while.

'Let's go find something to eat,' he suggested. 'I don't like this kind of nonsense food, as my father used to call it.'

'What did your father consider real food then?' she asked smiling.

'Well, he was a farmer. He liked good, simple food, on a plate, at a table. He didn't hold with walking around and eating, or just as bad, balancing your plate in your lap.' Sam smiled and she noticed that he had a very attractive, large, well-shaped mouth. He was altogether a tall, sturdy sort of man, and she could imagine him growing up in the country eating good country food.

They found a small restaurant near to the hotel and fell into an easy conversation. He talked about growing up in the country and winning a scholarship to go to university. She talked about growing up in the city with loving but strict church-going parents. She mentioned meeting Horace at university and marrying him but she felt uncomfortable talking about Horace, it seemed disloyal somehow. Sam was not married, couldn't afford it on his university salary, he joked, but really there had been someone serious, but he had been so wrapped up in his research, she had grown tired of waiting for him to emerge from his books and his lab and she had gone off and married someone else.

'A nice, respectable businessman,' he finished and laughed.

'Weren't you at least a bit heartbroken?' she asked.

'Oh yes, at the time. I was quite a mess,' and he changed the subject.

107

'See you're married to a businessman, wealthy, well known. I'm sure you would not have hung around waiting for a research student to surface.'

'Well, of course, I would have, if I had been in love with him. And anyway,' she added and wondered why she sounded a bit defensive, 'he wasn't wealthy and well known then.'

'In love!' Sam pretended to be horrified. 'That's obsolete these days.'

'And just as well,' thought Nellie. She wondered what it was, that thing, so many years ago, that had taken her into a marriage, into having children and had now left her, adrift in a city she did not know with a man she did not know.

They lingered over coffee. 'I think I have had too much to drink and to eat,' she said.

'Let's walk around for a while then,' he said. And so they did.

The street was full of shops, brightly lit and they strolled around, looking into shop windows, deciding on the merits of various bits of furniture, high-tech appliances. At a dress shop, Sam pointed out a dress that he thought she would look good in. It was bright green and cut low at the bosom.

Nellie laughed. 'You must be mad. I would never wear something like that. I'm much too old.'

'Come on,' he laughed, 'you're not old and you have a terrific figure.'

'God,' she thought, suddenly acutely uncomfortable, 'I hope he's not trying to flirt. It's too ridiculous. He's at least ten years younger than me.' From time to time, there had been men, usually balding, raunchy, paunchy, who tried to make a pass at her. She thought it grotesque.

'Perhaps we should get back,' she said, turning in the direction of the hotel.

'Hey,' he said. 'Now you're all uptight with me. Why? I haven't had such a good evening in a long time. To be honest, I'm not often very comfortable with women. Mostly I don't know what to talk about. Its the damned tapeworms. I mean, it hardly makes for the start of a glamorous and romantic conversation.'

She laughed and they were comfortable with each other again.

108

'That's what it is,' she thought later, alone in her room. 'Comfort, a feeling that I can say whatever I want. He doesn't know me in any other place or time.' And so she drifted comfortably towards sleep, surprised by the newness of it all, that she could be friends with a man.

They met the next afternoon, it was cool and sunny and they went walking in the park.

'We should see something of the city,' she said. 'But it's so nice not to be sitting in a cold conference room, not to be on a schedule. It's good to be moving about.'

'I've decided to accept their offer,' he said. 'I'm to move here by the end of the month.'

She said congratulatory things, she said they must celebrate, but she began to feel unaccountably sad. 'Because I won't see him again,' she thought. 'How foolish I am.' He also grew quiet. He had never lived abroad before. What if he hated it, couldn't bear the winter? She said reassuring things, it would be an adventure, meeting new people, making new friends, he would love it, she said. She thought she sounded much as she had when her children were going off to college and had a last minute panic about going. She had said the same sort of things later, organizing their tickets, their luggage, taking them to the airport. Only, watching their heads disappear into the departure lounge, she felt that she had said all the wrong things, she had sent them away when she wished desperately for them to stay.

Sam was saying that he was worried about leaving his mother, since his father died the previous year, she was on her own too much. But then his married sister was near by. She would visit. Nellie thought he was talking about her. She imagined herself with a pink knitted bed-jacket, like her Grandmother wore. Her Grandmother had come to live with them, she was sweet but muddled things and her mother was exasperated to find the soap in the fridge and the milk jug perched precariously on the edge of the bath. She snapped when Nellie giggled. Just you be careful, young lady, one day you'll be old, it's no laughing matter. No, indeed it was not. But she must stop this, he wasn't talking about her, it was her children, years from now, having this conversation, perhaps with respective husbands and wives, perhaps in a park like this, miles away from home. No, no, it wasn't that at all, she was walking in a park with someone who was talking about an old woman whom she did not know. She shivered.

The sun had gone in. They found a small café and stopped for a drink.

'What's wrong?' he asked.

'I don't know,' she said.

She was like her mother, she thought. Always trying to put things away neatly. A bit compulsive. Well, whatever the magazine articles said, it had worked. She was not neurotic. She was not one of those women who fell apart for no reason. She started talking. She told Sam about her children, how bright they were, how beautiful. Her parents did not hold with talk about physical appearance, one should be neat and tidy. Vanity was the work of the devil, they said. But she liked to tell her children that they were lovely. Perhaps she had made a mistake.

Sam was lost, he did not know how to calm her and so he listened and poured her more whisky. Perhaps she was ill. Perhaps he should take her back to the hotel. He wondered what was really bothering her.

'Why don't you tell me what's bothering you?'

'I don't know,' she said.

She allowed herself to be taken back to the hotel.

'The thing is,' she said abruptly, 'we have nothing in common. I'm saying goodbye to all sorts of things. I've given up on my marriage, said goodbye to my children and I'm disheartened by my job. All the things that mattered most to me are somehow over. And you are just starting things, a whole new phase in your life. It depresses me.'

He left, closing the door quietly.

It was the day for touring the major aid agencies. Displays and presentations had been arranged. It was important that she go

110

but she could not get up. She felt paralysed, a total absence of will. She couldn't even say that she was ill. She simply could not face leaving the room. Horace was due back home today. She called home but no one answered. But of course, the plane came in at mid-day, and with the time difference, it was much too early to be calling. It worried her that she had not thought about the time, she must be losing it, going funny in the head. Well what would she say to him anyway. There was a habit of not saying things that lay between them now. She had nothing to say to anyone. She had wasted her time saying things in conferences and now there was nothing left to say.

Sam telephoned. 'Get out of bed this minute and come and have breakfast with me.'

She laughed. 'I don't eat breakfast and I just had a moment of great illumination. I have nothing to say to anyone anymore.'

'Oh shit,' he said. 'Room 404 and I expect you here in five minutes.'

She went.

He poured coffee and she started to say something.

'No,' he said. 'You don't have to talk.'

And she didn't.

'Why do you bother?' she asked.

He took away her cup and kissed her. He felt strange. She did not know his mouth or his arms. 'I do not want to be unfaithful,' she thought. 'I want to keep things as they are. I don't want to be like Horace, to have sex that doesn't matter to me.' And then she knew that she had been keeping this as a sort of superiority. But also, she knew that even though her marriage had been so far from the sort of ideal she had envisaged, she had kept a feeling about what it should be. She needed to hold on to that.

He kissed her and stroked the back of her neck and suddenly she was leaning against him and she knew that she wanted them to be like that, relaxed, intense, comforting each other.

Afterwards she thought, 'Now it will be worse, I will feel even more bereft.'

But he made her laugh. He teased her about all sorts of things and then paid her extravagant, sexy compliments, so that she laughed again and fell asleep beside him. They spent the day like that, laughing, chatting, making love, vowing that they would get up and go out, but they stayed there as time telescoped itself around them.

On 'the Hill' decisions had been made, the go-betweens had spent a hectic day lobbying for this cause or that and the media houses would have much to report the next day. In fashionable Georgetown, little dinner parties were underway with guests enthusing about the 'nouvelle cuisine' even though many hoped there were leftovers waiting in the fridge for them at home, basic meat and potatos leftovers that would fill the gap left by the delicate, over-decorated food on their plates. On 16th Street the hookers went out into the night, happy that the weather had turned warm and that they could show off their minis without risking pneumonia. Their pimps, cruising by with the constellation of needle marks on their arms suitably hidden under leather jackets, smiled. Several conferences were on in town and business would be brisk. Professionals commuting out to Maryland, the schools were so much better there, hoped their wives and husbands would be on time to meet them at the station as it was a good night on TV. Washington got on with its life and they, immune to it all, got on with theirs.

They were due to leave on different flights. She could not bear to say goodbye. She insisted that he must not contact her when they were home. She did not want to be involved in an affair, all those lies and roundabout ways of meeting. He insisted that they must see each other. No, he was aware of her position, he did not want her to be embarrassed. But he must see her, even just once.

He left. She packed up her conference things. She made a polite call to the funding agency, made excuses for having missed the tour. She was fortunate to get through to a very chatty young man who was making his way to the top and was only too happy to show off his knowledge by giving her a detailed account of the agency's likely funding pattern. She heard it all, she made notes. It meant nothing to her.

She was surprised that she felt no guilt then anguished that perhaps she would be one of those women who are forever on the prowl for young lovers. She laughed at herself for thinking in stereotypes. She longed to see him, she thought about him constantly. How could she face Horace? Would he know? He must, she was so changed. She always knew when he had a new woman in his life.

But Horace was busy, he did not notice anything strange about her. He had found a beautiful insurance executive. She was black, very slim but with unexpectedly large, round breasts. He had worked his way into her apartment and into her blouse when she moved his hand away and asked, 'But what would you say if a man was propositioning your wife this way?'

'Oh no, but she's an intellectual, married to her work,' he said.

And the insurance executive threw his hand off her lovely, swelling breast and threw his person out of her beautifully decorated apartment.

But fate was good to Horace and by the very next day he was in another apartment with another executive. This time he did not allow her time for questions. Her breasts were not as splendid but he did the talking as he stroked them and worked his other hand between her thighs.

'It's all a matter of good choice and good luck,' he later told one of his Friday buddies who was moaning about his lack of success with a particular woman.

'There is so much to choose from. If she won't have you, believe me there are others who will. Just work fast and talk pretty, don't give her a chance to start asking questions and raise all sorts of doubts. Fatal man, to give a woman a chance to use her mind instead of her hormones.'

Nellie did not return Sam's calls although she thought about him constantly and wanted desperately to see him. At home she went into a fit of house cleaning, disturbing the contents of cupboards that had long lain comfortably hidden. At work her secretary was exhausted by her demands that everything be properly coded, filed, the smallest detail attended to in a specific way. And so she tried, unsuccessfully, to erase that one anarchic day but it lay there, clear in every detail, pulsating with a life of its own. When she read in the newspapers that he had joined the highly regarded international research agency and had left for Washington, she was almost glad. Now she would forget and things would return to normal.

Horace continued to weave elaborate fictions around his evenings until, exasperated, she begged him to stop.

'I don't care,' she said. 'Don't you understand that? I simply don't care anymore.'

At first he thought it was bravado, then he realized that she meant it and he became depressed. He stopped going out every evening. He stopped his long drinking bouts with the 'boys', those paunchy, middle-aged business executives with whom he had spent years of Friday nights. Unaccustomed to seeing so much of him, she avoided him. She took work home and spent the evenings feeding data into her computer. This dreary impasse lasted so long that at last she became ill and she decided to spend a week in the country to recuperate. He insisted that he would go with her. She insisted that she needed to be alone. She spoke of divorce and he went into fits of rage and grief. She dropped the subject.

Nellie went to a cottage by the sea. She couldn't bear to think that she was pining over such a very brief affair. Was it all about sex, she wondered and her mind went backwards and forwards over that question. Could she admit it, if that was it. Could the upbringing that led her not to be able to answer that truthfully be the other side of the coin for Horace, the reason why he had to explore and taste and move on again. And if that was it, could any of it be changed. And if so, changed to what? All she wanted, she thought, was to be able to feel something again. Anything. Anger even. But at what. At missing something? At missing out on something? 'Perhaps I lacked imagination,' she thought, 'some concept of how it could have been different.'

114

Before she left, she had been to see a doctor. He was about her age, with little touches of grey in his hair, he was handsome and disinterested in her symptoms. Peri-menopausal involuted melancholia, he called it, there was nothing to be done. It would sort itself out. When? A year or two perhaps. Good God, a year or two! Involuted melancholia, it sounded like the botanical name of some small, wild flower, a pretty, unnoticed little thing which researchers would later discover to have the cure for some unpleasant disease.

She was angry with him, his sublime disinterest sickened and infuriated her. Could he ever imagine having his whole life turned inside out, not by events but by the workings of his own body. She was angry with women who would consult such a man, be condescended to by such a man who knew only text-book symptoms. Such a foolish, old-fashioned sort of word, melancholia. She would have nothing to do with such a word.

Nellie gazed out of the window to the sea. She could hear its soft crashing on the rocks and smell the faint, salty smell of it. How blue the sky was. Two women and a child were walking on the shore. They made a small, close unit out there. Friends. She put on an old pair of shorts and went out to the beach. She passed two young men who made crude and detailed offers of their sexual favours. Her body might be making its own plans inside her, she thought, but apparently the word was not yet out. She felt a wave of anger at them, these lazy young boys who knew nothing about women, knew only their own need, their own masculine ego lusts, their blind assumption, a woman alone needs sex. And did she, did they? She thought of Horace's various conquests with a sudden tenderness, she hoped they had not been hurt, these women, any of them. She hoped they had been happy, able to take him or leave him as their bodies dictated.

The two women walked by her and stopped to chat. Tourists off the beaten track. Wasn't it gorgeous here, wasn't it all just heaven, they could not believe that a place like this really existed. God, such a change from Chicago and its miserable weather. They tossed their limp, blonde hair that had been braided and

115

showed tender patches of pink scalp. Their tanned, aerobically trimmed bodies exuded health and exuberance. The little girl with them was from the nearby fishing village and she had simply attached herself to them. Nellie felt herself smiling and talking, responding to their enthusiasm. She invited them to her cottage for a drink and they sat there on the verandah chatting, learning each other's life histories while the child lay curled up close beside her on an old-fashioned verandah swing. When it was almost dark they stood up to leave, the women were travelling the next day but the child said she would come back. Nellie was amused at how readily the child picked her up to fill the space that the two women would leave. The women were also amused but slightly hurt and perhaps, in their heart of hearts, slightly relieved that they would not have to feel that she was their responsibility.

The child's name was Patsy and she could not understand Nellie's wish to be alone. She wandered about the house, looked at magazines and stayed all day. At first Nellie ignored her, then she cooked a meal and they ate together. Patsy was not very communicative but she had an odd way of seeming to relax utterly into this new attachment until Nellie took it for granted that she would be there, first thing in the morning, when she opened the door. If she took a nap in the day, she would wake up to find Patsy curled up on the bed, like a little kitten, Nellie thought, seeking warmth. 'Where's your Mother, Patsy? Won't she be worried about where you've been all day?'

'Mama live in town, Miss. I live wid me Granny. She only say, "you behave yourself a good girl Patsy".'

But Patsy troubled her, her easy affection, her non-connectedness to anyone in her family. She must soon return to Kingston and what would happen to the child? She had brought up her children, she did not plan to start again. What was she to do about this child? She gnawed and fretted over the question, like a dog with a bone. She could not make a decision about her because she had not made one of her own. What would she do when she returned? The house, Horace, the job? It all seemed to be someone else's life and it didn't interest her. How had it all

116

become so empty and pointless? A friend of hers had said, 'What is it Nellie? You don't seem to be yourself lately.' And that was exactly it. She was not herself because she realized that she had been living as a 'self' that was unsatisfactory, incomplete. The things that she had thought made her a complete, well-rounded person, were in fact just so much activity. She had developed out of fragments, conditioning, sets of ideas about what a successful woman was.

'And perhaps the same thing has been happening to Horace too,' she thought. 'We don't know what is truly authentic, what is truly the self of each other.'

The day before she was to leave the cottage, Patsy came to her house much later than usual. Her face was shining and she was grinning from ear to ear.

'Me Daddy send for me. Him said him would! Me goin to live wid him in Merika.'

'So when will you go?' Nellie asked, astounded by such a turn of events. She had never heard mention of a Daddy.

'Soon, soon,' she said. 'Me Granny gone to town to look bout passport fe me. She tek me to tek pikture dis mornin.'

Nellie drove her into the nearest small town and bought her some new clothes and shoes to take to Merika. When they parted that evening, she watched the small figure with her shopping clutched to her chest, making its way down the narrow road.

'Bye girl,' she whispered, 'walk good.'

Nellie packed her things and tidied the cottage. The tears seemed to be endless, they had an unstoppable source of their own. At last she fell into bed exhausted. The next morning, out of habit she went to open the door for Patsy, but she wasn't there. She stood there, staring at the step for a long while then abruptly she went inside, made herself a cup of coffee and sat out on the verandah looking out at the sea. How had she not noticed the colours before, such blues and greens. Patsy had wanted a card with hair clips of all sorts of different colours. Nellie had thought they should try to get colours to match the dresses they had bought but it was the only thing that Patsy had asked for and she bought it. The shopkeeper had put it in a little brown paper bag and Patsy had clutched it as if it were a prized possession. Nellie smiled and something in her lifted and winged its way out towards the sea. Sam and Patsy, she hadn't sought for them, they hadn't asked anything of her. Thoughts of them moved round and round, forming intricate coloured patterns in her head.

The two boys from the beach passed by on the road below the cottage.

'Hi, nice lady, coming for a walk today?'

She smiled, shook her head and they waved and walked on.

'Time to get going,' she thought. She packed her things into the car, locked the cottage and set off. In the little fishing harbour, boats were coming in with the morning catch and she thought with a wave of urgency, 'They're coming back and I'm just setting out.'

She turned on the car radio, turned it up loud and belted her way into town.

Through a Glass Darkly

Ooee baby, baby you're so fine
I'd like to make you mine oh mine
oh baby, baby, baby you're so fine.

Soft, breathy voice. He was towelling off after the shower and he
could hear her singing in the bedroom. In the mirror he saw the
open door and beyond that the bed. She was lying on her back,
her arms around a pillow, legs stretched long and shapely among
the crumpled sheets. He walked into the room and she gazed at
him, absently, crooning to herself, then her eyes focused on
him and a spark, pinpoints of light came up in the depths of her
eyes.

'You're such a child,' he said affectionately, as he put on his
shirt.

The night was cool and dark and he drove slowly, relaxed,
contented. As he turned into his driveway he saw that a potted
plant on the verandah was smashed, the roots of the plant still
clinging stubbornly to clumps of earth, lay half in, half out of the
pot.

'Damn dogs,' he thought.

He let himself in quietly. Sylvie stirred as he got into bed
beside her.

'What have they broken this time? Damn dogs,' she said as
she turned away from him and buried her face in the pillow.

*

The world was sleeping. Magda lay breathing in the familiar smell of the man who had just left her bed.

Pwow . . . pwow . . . gunshots in the night.

She lay still. They sounded so close, but they probably came from several streets away. That's how it is in the night, she thought. She listened to every sound then. Plop. A ripe mango fell from the tree just outside her window. Her heart raced and she felt hot. Pwow . . . pwow . . . more gunshots. Then silence.

A cup of tea, a cigarette. Drinking tea like this, late at night always reminds her of England. Having babies in an English hospital. The nurses bustle around so early in the morning it's still dark, and wake the women up with cups of tea. Strong taste, hot and fragrant in a thick white cup. In the cool ward a slight steam rises from the cup into her face. Her body feels strong and relaxed until she moves to put down the cup and her arm brushes against a breast. Monstrous, swollen, painful things, grotesque mounds jutting out from her body.

Her baby has a bright, wide awake look, her head strong, a mass of jet black hair crowns her head so that she looks like a little Indian. Magda laughs at the large, pugnacious nose. When the babies are wheeled into the ward, the basinettes tethered beside their mother's beds, she can see her baby's nose, there among the sea of pale, soft-faced babies. Holding her, that first morning Magda thought only, I will love you for ever and ever.

The baby was hungry and set up a loud cry. The English mothers looked over briefly. This dark, wide-awake baby was not to be ignored. Gathering her up, Magda put her to the breast. The baby sucked and stopped and set up a loud, lusty complaint and a nurse came bustling over.

Nurse was a big, sturdy young woman with heavy blonde hair pulled back under her cap so that her face looked smooth and naked. Cornish farming family, Magda thought. Thick milk and clotted cream and the salty smell of the sea.

Nurse took the baby away and came back with a small bottle. 'Now dear, we're going to get some of that milk out. Engorged we are, aren't we. Now we'll just take it out, put it in this little bottle and baby won't know the difference will she. Real little fighter that one,' said Nurse pulling the curtains around Magda's bed and slipping the shoulders of her nightgown down in one smooth movement. 'Have to pad the sides of her basinette in the nursery. That one, she's moving around so much.' The soft West country burr was comforting. Nurse gave her the bottle to hold and stood slightly behind her. With both hands she massaged firmly in a downwards movement, her hands warm with a rough edge on one finger.

'I'm a cow,' Magda thought. 'She's milking me just like a cow.'

After what seemed like hours a few thin drops of liquid fell reluctantly into the bottle.

My body was a private thing, she thought. She had not liked sex, not liked being touched and looked at as if she was owned. When he came at her in the nights she wanted to say, leave me alone, I want my privacy, my body is my own. But she did not say it because he said he loved her. And if a man loves you he wants to touch you and be inside your body. And she did not like to touch his body, but she liked his affection and because she liked that, he had access to her private body. And now a baby had come out of that body and a woman was milking her like a cow.

Nurse gave up on the right breast. She laid a warm cloth on it and started in on the left one. She massaged and massaged and squeezed the nipple. A few drops joined the small smudge of liquid in the bottle.

Tears were flowing down Magda's face.

'Please stop,' she whispered. Polite Magda, even in pain.

Nurse gave up, exhaling a little sigh of vexation. 'It's a crying shame,' she said, looking at the veined, monstrous things. 'So much milk there, and we'll have to give her the bottle.'

There it was out. The ultimate admission of failure. Magda was crying, her nose red. Nurse went away and came back with the baby and a bottle of formula. The baby sucked greedily at the bottle, the tiny fingers of one hand spread elegantly, daintily over a swollen breast.

Magda finished her tea and went upstairs to bed. She slept and dreamed of her second baby. Spiky black hair and slanted, navy blue eyes, a lotus blossom bloom on her. 'I will love you for ever and ever,' she said to this new, beautiful baby. She nursed her babies and they fell asleep close beside her.

Sylvie watched him getting dressed to go to work. The whole damned island may be falling apart but every morning he showered and dressed in a correct suit with a suitable tie. He drank his coffee black, had some fruit, for he was slightly vain and dreaded putting on middle-age spread, talked to her about their son who was to start tennis lessons that day, what time she was to take him, who to ask for, the receipt for the lessons he had paid for, and then he was gone, the children rushing to get their school things together and pile into the car with him.

A neat, organized man she thought. Growing up in a poor, hopelessly muddled household, she liked that about him. But she was glad he was gone. How irritating these instructions were becoming. As if she had no sense. Once in charge of a whole department at Williams and helping him with all his various projects. But as he progressed, she regressed, had to be instructed in all sorts of simple things. She sighed. He was a good man, just getting to be rather dull and pompous. She wished she could get away for a while. She poured herself a cup of coffee and lit a cigarette. He disliked her smoking and she only did so occasionally, when he wasn't around, but now she inhaled deeply and looked out at the large, well-kept garden. Last night she had heard the dogs racing around and what sounded like a flower pot breaking. It infuriated her that every night the neighbour's dogs used her garden as a race track and no matter how she fixed the fence, they always found some way to get in. She'd have to have Nathan check the fence again today. And get a lock for the gate. The damn mango tree, it should have been a blessing, something they could enjoy and enjoy giving the fruit away. But these days, it had become a curse. The little boys were one thing, now it was men, sauntering in, stripping the tree and leaving the skins and

122

seeds all over the place. No respect for anything or anyone, nothing was private any more. Her thoughts raced around, disjointed, the children to collect at school and get to their various activities, why was he so often late, dinner for some friends out from New York, perhaps she'd make a cake, well he was moving up so quickly, manager of his branch now, she must re-pot that plant, she should take up a hobby, plants were good business, but he would take it over, tell her how to run it. She stubbed out the cigarette. What was happening to her, when did she start thinking like this? They were happy. Sylvie got up and started her day.

In her small back garden, the pear tree had grown large and shapely, covered in blossoms that promised a bumper crop. Only, as usual, there would be no crop. It was a stupid place for the landlord to have planted a tree, too small a space and so many electric wires criss-crossing the yard. Magda had arranged for a gardener to come and she instructed him anxiously.

'Mind yourself now, you hear. Don't go near the wires.'

And for the hour that he was there chopping away at the shiny leaves, she locked herself away in the house, tense and worried about the man and the tree. But there were no flashes of electricity, no screams. He was there, reassuringly familiar, a small wiry man in baggy old trousers, wielding his machete in smooth, curving chops. He hauled the branches away and the back of the house was flooded with sunlight and he raked the blossoms up in pale, neat piles.

The house was empty and quiet and full of light. That night she would tell him. It's not right. Stay away. It's all wrong. Don't come back. I hate the sound of the guns at night but you always go. Stay away then. She looked at the raw, ragged edges of the tree and wept that she could be so destructive.

The days passed. And the nights. She tried to tell him. But he was steady, remarkably obstinate. They had been lovers for a long time and they suited each other very well, he said. She laughed at the way he said it, for they did not speak of love but he had helped her to change and now she loved him sexually, the smell of him, his strong, heavy body all around her. And perhaps, she thought, listening to his quiet breathing beside her, this deep sexual attachment was as valid as any other form of love. Freely given, with a remarkable quality of honesty. But later, when she heard him in the shower, she thought of the water coming from high up in the hills, flowing under green leaves, over smooth, pale stones that trembled and touched each other as the water passed, and she resolved once again, to put an end to it.

'It's not right,' she said eventually. 'You must not come back.'

'As you wish,' he said this time. 'I don't want you to be unhappy.'

The kite flying days of Easter were over and it was hot even at night. The city had grown and grown, up into the hills, out along the coast and it seemed as if this thick, untidy growth had blocked off the air, used up the water, formed a barrier to the sea breezes. She planned a picnic in the mountains with some friends. It rained and they did not stay long but packed their things up and left as mist was beginning to move towards them. Its lovely, she said, we needn't go yet. You're crazy, they said, who wants to sit around in the rain. She began to have an odd, terrifying sensation of falling, falling into a dark endless space and she stopped going out, except to work. At home she turned on the fan and in the soft whirring she thought of birds, wings light in the air, over a mountain, catching the up-current over a stream. She saw the flash of their reflection in the moving water and looked up, away from the dark space. She was busy, she said, if anyone called, but really she was dreaming of the Italian lake district, of geographically imprecise green valleys flecked with daisies, of a Japanese house and beyond, an austere Zen garden.

In the office there were endless meetings. Devaluation, deregulation, all sorts of new regulations and taxes to be paid. The accountant brought out sheets of computer paper, ruled in green. They would have to increase the price of the product, trim the wage bill, if they were to improve the bottom line. It was the time honoured response to trouble.

Madga outlined alternatives. The accountant took off his spectacles and tapped the end of an arm delicately against his new bridgework. 'It's not that simple,' he said condescendingly. He replaced his spectacles and went back to the spreadsheet.

She knew she had lost. For years they had been running things that way and for years they had made a healthy profit. The bottom line was now a real thing, it sat grinning impudently at her. The workers were not real, their faces, their families, their children at school, their mortgaged homes, they did not appear on the pale green lines.

In the past, she had won some and lost some, she would fight this one out too. But back in her office Magda felt weary. She moved pieces of paper into neat piles. In. Out. She stapled edges together, such a clean, satisfying click sound the stapler made as she bound corners together and secured them in a file. There, a mark that someone had done something today. The managers were afraid. They were afraid because they believed in a limited world. I have a car and a house but there are not enough for you to have. At night the TV fed their fears, showed them the homeless children, boys sleeping on the street at night, begging for money in the day.

'Beg you a Concorde,' the child's eyes close up against her car window, his face full of flirtatiousness.

'A what!' She laughed. A Concorde, the new $100 bill, so lacking in value it flew out of your pocket. 'My you bright,' she said and gave him a $2 bill.

He grinned, grabbed the bill and stepped smartly out of the traffic as the lights changed.

The TV cameras cut from the smart, well-dressed announcers to city scenes, rural scenes, anger and poverty everywhere. The managers in the corporate corridors closed ranks against this have-not world. Magda closed the filing cabinet and walked out of the building. She got into her car and headed out of the city. Fat cats, she thought. Fat cats and lean cats, mean cats and alley cats. I hate fur, hate cats, their mewling, treacherous ways.

She was on a curving country road, the sides gorged out by recent flood rains. Careful, she thought, suicide brings the worst karma. A truck lumbered around a corner straight at her and she pulled the car sharply into the bank. The truck passed within an inch of her car and as she looked up she could see the truck driver's face, gazing impassively at her in his rear view mirror. She pulled out slowly, scraping the side of the car. A reflex, to swerve away from the truck, not even thought about, that pull of the wheel away from that big, welcoming truck.

The sea is warm, body warm. Temperature of amniotic fluid. Magda was floating, the sun warm against her face, her body buoyed up by the water. She remembered her first communion dress. The veil over her face made everything in the church seem watery. A tree with yellow blossoms grew beside the window and the gold wash of colour came into the church. She felt beautiful, blessed, in her white dress, a bride of Christ. But the priest was warning them against sins of commission and omission and she turned her eyes away from the tree into the grey, gloom of the church and the figure of the man, dressed in long, ornate robes, his face and voice forbidding, way up in a dark wooden pulpit.

There was shouting somewhere. She half-opened her eyes against the afternoon glare and turned over on her stomach, treading water. The voices were coming from the beach which seemed to be a long way away. Some children were standing there calling to someone. A woman bobbed up in the water beside her.

'Come in now,' she shouted.

Magda swam in, following the woman. She was so tired, her arms could barely move, her eyes were burning. The woman nudged her awake. They swam, for ever it seemed. Magda felt herself thin and weak, the water heavy, resisting, but then she was seized with a flash of energy, she swam strongly with the other woman matching her strokes, arm over arm in a strong,

126

regular rhythm until at last they tumbled in a wave on to the beach. Magda lay gasping, her eyes closed against the sun. Hands pulled her up into a sitting position and pushed her head forward. She retched and spat up hot, salt water, then she was cold, so very cold and tired.

It was night, dark all around. She looked towards the window for the glow of the streetlight near her house. Nothing, and the window wasn't in the right place. She sat up and realised, I'm not in my room, not in my bed. She got out of bed and walked unsteadily over to the one wooden louvred window and opened it fully. Hills, no lights anywhere but a pale moonlight slipped into the room and quiet everywhere. A bed, a chair, a chest of drawers. A small, empty room. Magda climbed back into bed trying to remember. The beach, children shouting, a woman swimming, she fell asleep again.

Early in the morning she woke again. The woman brought her a cup of tea.

'Thank you,' said Magda. ' Is my baby awake yet?'

But the woman, who wasn't a nurse said, 'My name is Estelle. Do you remember yesterday on the beach?'

'Yes, I'm sorry.'

'Suicide brings the worst karma,' said Estelle.

'Yes, I know. I was trying to go towards something.'

'Drink your tea,' said Estelle. 'I must go to work. We'll talk when I get back.' She turned away. A tall, heavy set woman with a thick, black plait that hung over one shoulder.

Magda drank the tea, how good it tastes, she thought.

For several hours she slipped in and out of sleep. She was in a crowded hall. A man was playing the piano, something modern, frantic, discordant. She was tense, trapped by the ugly sounds but a small child beside her sat quite still throughout it and Magda felt ashamed of her own irritability and restlessness. A woman in the row in front of her was wearing ear-rings, thin gold chains which ended in blue, glass spheres. Magda gazed at them and slowed her breathing, calming herself with the unexpected colour. A wonderful shade of blue, the colour of Mary's robes in a stained glass window and she felt herself slipping through the

127

blue glass and she was a child in a big church, praying for forgiveness. 'What have I done?' she wondered. Anguished, the child prayed over and over, 'I'm sorry, forgive me, forgive me . . .'

Magda shivered in the hot hall. Distracted she looked away from the woman with the glass ear-rings. Beside the woman was an elderly man, the back of his neck wrinkled like an old shoe. He wore thick spectacles. He turned his head suddenly and through a corner of them she could see french windows open, latecomers sat there, listening attentively. The outsiders, double filtered through the spectacles, through the windows, swam there, pressed up close to the window. She seemed to see the man sitting there with his wife and children. All of them neat, well-dressed, a pleasant correctness hung over them. Through a glass darkly, she thought. But it wasn't like that at all, it was very clear.

Magda woke again to find Estelle standing by the bed. 'Do you feel well enough to get up? I've fixed some soup.'

She got up and realized that she was wearing an old nightgown, sizes too big for her.

'I have no clothes,' she said, suddenly self-conscious.

Estelle smiled. Her face was a deep copper colour and Magda realized, from the quality of light on her face and in the room that it must be afternoon.

'Mine will be no use to you,' said Estelle. 'It doesn't matter anyway, it's just us.'

The house was small, sparsely furnished. They must be far out in the country somewhere, it was so quiet. They sat at a plain wooden table and Estelle brought two large bowls of soup and a plate of bread. Magda ate, savouring the hot, slightly peppery taste of the soup.

Estelle said, 'What's your name?'

'Magda,' she answered, not wanting to talk.

'Ah,' said Estelle and burst out laughing. 'Mary Magdalene, the sinful woman with her perfumed ointments.'

A sort of fear took hold of her. The house was so quiet, she could hear her own breathing. Perhaps the woman was mad, some kind of religious fanatic.

128

'No, no,' she said, trying to sound light-hearted. 'My mother's name was Margaret, my father's name was David. They put the names together, that's all. It really has no other significance.'

'He loved Mary Magdalene, you know,' Estelle continued as if she hadn't spoken. 'The woman of spiritual intuition and sensuality. The disciples were frightened by such a woman, far better Mary the Virgin, the passive receptacle to carry the boy child. That's why the church developed the way it did. All oppressive male heirarchy, all sorts of structures and robes to cover up things and all sorts of nonsense to keep us out and admit us mainly in our Martha role. Dependable workers, church cleaners.'

Perhaps she's an ex-nun, bitter about something, Madga thought, and we're alone here. I don't even know where I am.

'I'm sorry Estelle,' she said. 'I'm not much of a church goer really. Well, not any more. You've been very kind but I should go now.'

Estelle smiled. 'It's OK, I'm not mad and I'm not going to preach at you, it's just that it's quite a coincidence. I'd been thinking how hard it is to keep the various personas going and I'd gone to the beach to forget about it, get on to some other wavelength, you know what I mean.' She shrugged slightly as if to dismiss the subject. 'The name suddenly made the thought come clear, that's all. I think she should have stayed and fought, maintained a place in the church. Don't you?'

'Yes, but one gets tired of fighting, out of step all the time with the rest of the world, it seems.' said Magda. 'Yes I know I'm right, but I can't seem to make them understand. And then, somctimes I'm so wrong. I saw her through the glass, Sylvie, that is. She's pretty, the way her hair curls around her ears and her children are so neat and well-behaved, but she doesn't look happy. And each year the pear tree blossoms and I have to cut it, before it can bear. I'm sorry, I'm talking nonsense. Maybe I've been ill. It's been so hot.'

Estelle reached out and broke off a piece of bread. 'Have some. I bake it myself.'

Magda took the bread and ate it slowly. She was very still, as if everything in her had stopped moving, her blood had stopped flowing, her heart stopped beating.

'I'm so tired,' said Magda.

'Yes,' said Estelle quietly, 'that's how it is. We have to start over again from the beginning. Over and over again.'

Magda got up and went back to her room. An empty room, no possessions. Through the window she could see the quiet hills and a few stars far, far away. She fell deeply asleep.

The Cousin

Professor B said . . . 'yes well', the words cold, clipped, and yet another attempt at conversation withered and died. As visiting lecturer, I was being welcomed at a rather stilted soirée. We sipped glasses of sherry, a detestable drink at the best of times, and I felt as if I had never left England at all. Professor B initiated the various discussions, his colleagues in the English department responded in suitable manner and I was just about to make my escape when I was invited by the Professor, instructed would be a more accurate word, to be the other half of a two person panel, set up to make the final choice of submissions for the University English prize.

The prize consisted of a modest cash award but the real attraction was that the manuscript would be submitted to a university press in the USA. The two universities had a sort of 'gentleman's' agreement which almost assured the manuscript of publication.

As visiting scholar, the terms of my four months' stint were not onerous and I had looked forward to an escape from the rigours of a London winter and the in-fighting of my own university. A breather in the sun. I was given a cool, high-ceilinged house with louvre windows which opened out to a garden full of large trees and flowering bushes. In the house I could quickly forget that my colleagues were quite pleasant but thankfully reserved. I could avoid the advances of the English members of faculty who seemed to be either aggressively unhappy with everything local or just as aggressively unhappy with everything British and anxious to prove themselves more local than the locals.

131

The panel assignment, therefore, came as a disagreeable surprise. I dislike having to critique the work of young writers, in fact, I have been quoted as saying that the inclusion of 'creative writing' as a university course was a piece of folly and students would be better off getting to grips with reading a variety of literature. The writing would come later. Dismissed as the mutterings of an old fogey, I nevertheless continued to avoid any attempt to get involved in having to comment on the outpourings of such courses. However, I could not refuse the request, the directive really, of Professor B. I sensed that, should I decline, it would cause a major upset in the Department, and while I am not usually sensitive to such matters, I felt reluctant to create any unpleasantness right at the beginning of my stay.

The submissions had already been shortlisted to two and these I was given. I bore them off, in their blue bindings, to my study. Before I could start reading them, however, I had an invitation to dinner at the house of one of the faculty members. Dr Chen would shortly be visiting scholar at my university near London and he sent his wife, a small, nervous sort of woman, to collect me and take me to their home. There were two other couples and a single woman and the talk was mainly about department affairs. Not much different to home, I thought, and settled down prepared to mask my boredom with whatever modicum of good manners I could muster. However, I was not to be let off easily. The conversation turned to the English prize, and I quickly said that I had only just received the manuscripts that afternoon and had not yet read them.

'Save yourself the bother,' said a woman in flowing African robes. 'This is the third year that we have tried to award the prize and somehow nothing can get past Prof B.'

'Perhaps they were not of a good standard,' I said.

'Cho, if you believe that, you will believe anything,' she said, tossing her rather handsome head which had been almost shaved clean of hair.

I concentrated on getting the bones out of the fish on my plate and hoped that that would be the end of the matter.

A tall, thin Indian man ladled pepper sauce on to the already highly spiced fish and I recognized him as the lecturer who taught Shakespeare and contemporary American writers, quite a combination, I had thought, when we were first introduced.

'You think he's going to let any young student beat him into publication? His novel is still going the rounds, turning up rejection slips by the dozen.'

I gazed with some apprehension as he put a large forkful of fish and pepper into his mouth but he ate it with obvious relish. I gulped some water and said, with what I hoped was a pleasant but firmly dismissive tone, 'I haven't read them yet, so perhaps we should change the subject . . . not prejudice the hearing . . . so to speak.'

But they were off. They gossiped in a bored sort of way about the man and I found myself the unwelcome possessor of all sorts of personal information about the Professor. I could have been at home, I thought wearily. Those apparently listless but unerringly targeted remarks about wives, lovers, about lobbying for higher positions, all so depressingly familiar.

'Do stop,' I said, perhaps a bit too loudly.

There was an uncomfortable silence and Mrs Chen rushed to heal the breach with offerings of more fish, pale, splintered and congealing on its platter.

The conversation turned to safer topics and I took my leave as soon as I could decently organize it. Safe in my home, I opened all the windows and gazed out. In the distance, the mountains were a solid, reassuring mass. They had so surprised me, these rugged, encircling mountains, all colours of blue and green during the day, settling in to rich purple in the evening.

So much learning, so little wisdom. Paradise lies just beyond the window, would that a small corner of it could inhabit our minds.

Well, I have never had any literary ambitions and my diary is my small self-indulgence. But I surprise myself. The older I get, the simpler my thoughts and expressions of them. It is as if, having spent all my working life immersed in the writings of others, I can only now express myself in very unsophisticated terms.

133

The next morning I tackled the manuscripts. The first, 'Man a Yard' was difficult to read as great portions of it were written in the local dialect. I make no apologies for being somewhat of a purist in the matter of language and do not share my colleague Edward's enthusiasm for all the permutations of English now emanating from the former British colonies. The story was one of apparently endless and explicit sexual conquests, some naive political theories and a great deal of detail in matters of local food and popular culture. The novel was poorly constructed but it had a certain earthy immediacy and I found myself, for the first time, understanding, even somewhat envious of, the cocky, over-confident young black man who was the central character. Perhaps it was not the sort of novel which the University would be happy to recommend to its American university connection but it undoubtedly had the makings of a local best seller. It should not be ignored.

The second manuscript was entitled 'Free Fall' and from remarks made the previous evening, I knew it was written by a woman. I really do deplore the fact that young women writers have fallen into the confessional mode and pour out endless novels cataloguing their growing years with unpleasant details of the female maturation process. There would be the obligatory loss of virginity, marriage and divorce, topics which did not interest me in the least. My own marriage I now viewed as a sort of aberration of the otherwise quiet flow of my life. For four years I lived with a woman who allowed me no privacy, who was given to inexplicable emotional outbursts which I could not at all understand. They frightened me, these rages, these tears, and I was not sorry when she went off to Australia with a PhD student.

With some reluctance I began to read what promised to be yet another bildungsroman, a genre not suited to women. If grown women are perplexing, young girls are simply frightful. Who on earth needs to follow them through their schoolgirl frolics, their silly crushes and vapid little friendships. With a sigh I settled down to 'Free Fall'. The first paragraphs were extremely disturbing.

After one of those visits, I rush home, cut myself a chunk of bread, plaster it with honey and eat it slowly. I hadn't realized I was doing this, but now I catch myself, the knife dripping with honey in one hand, the other hand cramming sweetness and energy into my mouth. So childish. Trying physically to replace the bitter taste, the draining anguish of those visits to Mama C.

Sitting in her hot, cluttered room I would desperately try to think of something funny to say but my mind fell empty, a perfect, receptive void. She had an unstoppable font of ugly memories. She had catalogued all sorts of imagined slights, terrible things that people had done to her in the distant past. In her stories she always figured as kind, generous, loving and other people rewarded her virtues with unkindness. Sometimes drop by drop, sometimes in a stream, accompanied with weeping, she poured out her poison. It was the worst kind of abuse, this swamping of the last shred one might have of happy memories, this heavy-footed trampling of the past.

It all came flooding back to me. The dark, cool pantry, my finger deep in the honey jar and when I pulled it out I would watch the thick, viscous stuff flow back to fill up the space I had just made. In the winter the honey was thick and white, in summer it had more flow, more movement, more golden colour in its depths. I would lick my finger slowly, carefully, not liking the sweetness so much as the smoothness of it on my skin, my tongue.

I had not connected any of it with my entrapment with Aunt Lena, that childhood shredded by her tongue, her endless complaints, her suffocating unhappiness.

With reluctance I returned to the manuscript. The details of the story bore little resemblance to my own experiences and I tried to keep my distance from it, to emphasise in my own mind the differences. I had escaped from Aunt Lena into an ordered, academic world, but the central character in the novel had made all sorts of disastrous choices so that her life was a series of starts and stops, a circular movement leading nowhere. In another passage that caught my attention, the main character said:

> If she would not let me have any calm, untroubled memories, I would find some to claim. I would resurrect for myself some moments, no, whole passages of time, when the earth moved in a calm, well-ordered manner. I would find places of beauty, people who were kind, funny, even just plain boring, to fill those red gashes she had left in my past.

It was late afternoon when I finished reading 'Free Fall'. I pottered about in the kitchen, fixing myself something to eat and then I tried to settle down to mark some essays. I spent a troubled evening, my thoughts returning over and over again to Aunt Lena, her house, her voice. I was filled with a ridiculous desire to cry, to put my head down on this borowed desk, far from home, and weep.

The following afternoon I met with Professor B. He sat in a large, leather chair behind an imposing desk and I felt myself to be at a disadvantage, perched on a little metal chair which had been pulled up, attentive student style, to the desk. I suggested that we award the prize to 'Free Fall' and that I would recommend that the author of 'Man a Yard' submit a copy to my colleague Edward who could recommend a suitable publisher.

Professor B. arched an eyebrow and smiled. 'You're not serious. I had assumed, being a neo-classicist yourself that you would find little of interest in the work. Personally 'Man a Yard' borders on the pornographic and is, in my opinion, not the sort of work with which I would wish this department associated. The other . . .' he paused and gazed out of the window for a few moments, before reluctantly returning his attention to me. 'Quite well written . . . I don't deny that . . . but ultimately . . . isn't it a bit parochial . . . a bit provincial. Would it have any sort of wide appeal?'

I shrugged. 'Few writers were as provincial as Jane Austen. In any case, it is not up to us to make a publishing decision. The work has merit and I think we should recognize it.'

Professor B seemed to impute a touch of censure to my remark for he raised his chin and looked down at me along the length of his rather aristocratic nose.

'Well, of course,' he smiled, without warmth, 'I would not presume to judge what a publisher might or might not like.' He tidied up some books on his desk and looked at me dismissively. 'I will think about your recommendation and make a decision. I hear you went to the Chens' last night. Pleasant people aren't they. I quite envy them the time they have to socialize. My own schedule is so demanding.'

I stood up and headed for the door, determined not to be drawn into further unpleasantries and to recover some control of the situation. 'I believe that we are required to make a joint decision before the end of this month. Perhaps we can meet again next Thursday, say three o'clock, my office?'

I left, heartily wishing I was back in my own familiar surroundings. I did not want to be at odds with the Professor but the battle lines were now drawn and there seemed no way to avoid what would be yet another disagreeable meeting.

Walking back across the campus to my house, I thought again how I had, uncharacteristically, accepted the invitation to come here. Perhaps it was the prospect of my sixtieth birthday looming up this year which had shaken me into agreeing to such a move. I was used to my flat, my colleagues, the damp smell in the corridor between my study and the library, the snap of paper rolling into Miss Adams' typewriter in the office next door to mine. I was content, so why this ridiculous fling, this venture into territory not my own? Occupied with my own dour thoughts, I almost bumped into Carmen, the lecturer in African robes who I had met at the Chens'. We greeted each other and continued across the campus together towards the residential area. We were almost neighbours, her house being two doors away from mine.

'Come in and have some ginger beer,' she said. 'I made some last night. No, it's not alcoholic,' she added, perhaps sensing some slight reluctance on my part.

I went in with her and stared at her collection of local and

137

African art while she set out glasses with the strong tasting ginger beer. We sat talking for a while and I dreaded her asking me about the manuscripts but she said nothing about them and talked instead about some of the new books she would be teaching that term. I was not familiar with the work of the writers she admired and she lent me various books by local and African writers. 'I know it's not really your field,' she said, 'but since you're here, you might find them interesting. It's always been rather a one way trade, hasn't it?'

I was relieved when she changed the subject as I sensed a lecturette about to descend. She showed me around her garden and pointed out several flowering specimens of orchids which she had grown herself. After I left, I thought I should have invited her over to give me some advice on my own garden. It was becoming quite unkempt but I felt unequal to tackling it in the heat. Aunt Lena was marvellous with roses. Everyone remarked on her neat garden, the size of her blooms, the colour, the fragrance. But she suspected her neighbours of clipping her blooms, of getting new hybrids more exotic than her latest acquisition, just to annoy her. Gardens had bad associations for me.

I was annoyed with myself. Suddenly everything seemed to lead back to Aunt Lena and, having refused to think about her for so long, I now wondered how accurate my memories were. Perhaps, I was doing an Aunt Lena myself, distorting events, memories.

An opportunity soon presented for me to speak to Carmen about the garden and she turned up a few days later with a gardener in tow. Mr Anderson was a man of few words and after a brief consultation with Carmen he set to work with a machete on the bougainvillaeas.

I led the way back to the house and Carmen settled herself comfortably on a verandah chair.

'Sometimes,' she said, 'I wish I could just sit around not doing anything at all, just getting old and set in my ways.'

I think I said something gallant about her not being old enough to talk that way and it would be more true coming from me. I wished I could talk to her about the meeting looming up with Professor B that afternoon. But we spoke of other things and I enjoyed listening to her voice. She had studied and travelled in Africa, she liked being back in her island, but she was restless, time to go somewhere new. Get too settled and one gets ossified, she said. I thought her to be the least ossified person I had ever met. She was tall, plump and her robes flowed around her much as her conversation flowed from one subject to another.

I walked back with her to her gate and reluctantly went on to my meeting with Professor B. The meeting was as disagreeable as I had anticipated. He did not think that either manuscript should get the prize and he would not budge from his position. When I suggested that we get another opinion, perhaps from the Dean of the Faculty, he had several reasons why this was unsuitable.

We had reached an impasse. The Professor seemed to think that the matter was settled and rose to leave with a vague remark about hoping for better quality submissions the following year. I was angry. Angry that the Professor's colleagues had so correctly, if bitchily, summed up the situation and angry that I could not get past his intransigent position.

I returned wearily to my house and found Mr Anderson cleaned up and ready to leave.

'Thank you,' I said. 'You've done a fine job here.'

'Tanks,' he replied, looking slowly around the garden. 'Some people want to believe dat any and everybody dat don't have a job can turn gardener. I been a farmer for plenty years now, but when de crops not ready, I like to tek on a little gardening work. Like anyting, you have to know what you doing.'

I paid him and walked with him towards the gate.

'What do you do,' I found myself asking, 'when you find a plant that you don't know much about, the type of plant that gives a lot of trouble to grow.'

Mr Anderson stopped in his tracks and considered the question.

'Not too many plants I don't know bout. Most of dem, if you don't know dem demself, you know dem cousin. So you treat dem same way you would treat de cousin but you tek time get to know what dem want to thrive. Maybe cousin like plenty water, but him, he don' want too much. Just tings like dat you have to try till you get to know what an what him like.'

Mr Anderson opened the gate and let himself out. We agreed on a date for him to return and I watched his heavy-set body moving along the tree-lined road. I thought suddenly that we were probably about the same age but looking at the easy way he swung his body and the strong set of his shoulders, I felt pale and flabby and old.

It was so hot. I began swimming in the university pool and discovered that late afternoon was a good time to swim, the pool almost deserted with only the shouts of young footballers floating from the playing field across the road. I had never been much of an athlete, being self-conscious about being short and having rather bandy legs. But with no one about, I began to enjoy my afternoon sessions, surprised at how much I looked forward to increasing the number of laps I could do each afternoon.

After one of these sessions, I stopped at Carmen's house to invite her over for a drink.

'Well now,' she said smiling, 'look at who is beginning to look like a real somebody! You seem so much more relaxed.'

I still wasn't used to the sort of personal remarks which the island folk made, but I regarded it as a compliment. I looked like a real somebody, what an odd idea. She walked back to my house with me and we sat sipping rum and cokes on my verandah. Perhaps I wasn't yet quite used to the rum, but I found myself talking a great deal, eventually telling her about my failure with the Professor.

'Thought that would happen,' she said. 'I don't want to think he's just plain mean-spirited, but that's how it looks.'

Then I told her about Mr Anderson's advice. She was amused at my attempt to quote him with his mix of 'dem' and 'demself' and plants which were 'him' and had 'cousins'. Then she grew thoughtful. 'Well, I can't help you there. I thought he modelled himself after some idea of an English

140

Professor so you are more likely to know of a similar 'cousin' than I am.'

'No, no, I don't know much about people really . . . avoid them as much as possible, particularly English professors. I am the old eccentric in my department, I've earned the reputation and I make good use of it!'

Carmen laughed and stretched her plump, shapely arms. She wore several silver bangles which tinkled as she raised her arms and the sound of her laugh, mixed with the noise of the bangles, made a peculiarly feminine sound. A sound with which I was absolutely unfamiliar but which I found extremely arresting.

'Well, I think you are a very nice, old eccentric,' she said, 'particularly now that you are thawing out and making friends with yourself.'

Another odd expression, I thought looking away from her arms to her dark eyes and heavy, curved mouth.

'I have an idea,' she said. 'I'm sure you know people in publishing, perhaps you should forget about the prize and just send off the manuscripts without any further consultation with Prof.'

I found several arguments against such a course of action, not the least of which was that I would need to consult with the authors, whom I did not know. I suspect that there was a level at which I did not want to get involved with the future of these manuscripts. I had only a month left and then I would be back in England.

While I mumbled and muttered, Carmen sipped her drink and gazed out at the mountains. Finally, she drained her drink and set the glass on a small, bamboo table. 'I don't see why you're making such a producion of this,' she said. 'If you don't want to do it, forget it. In fact, I will start making some enquires myself and recommend some publishers to them. Thanks for the drink,' she added and turned to leave.

I had disappointed her. It was a most disturbing thought.

When I swim, I feel my arms moving in a strong pattern. I feel the slight resistance of the water and feel myself countering this, smoothly, without struggle. The process takes place somewhere in a balance between intellect and instinct, territory which I have not explored before. First I could only swim five laps, now I can swim ten, I am beginning to extend myself, to expect something of myself. This young writer, struggling with her Mama C, is trying not to fall into the poison, the nihilism, she is trying to expect something of herself and I am turning away from her. Perhaps, I am the Professor's cousin.

I really will not write any more in my diary. All of this probing and self-assessment was ridiculous. I threw myself with even more vigour into preparing for my lectures and into improving my swimming. I arranged to meet the two writers and made suggestions about publishing. They were cynical about the non-award of the prize and their cynicism extended to me. I felt them shutting me out and could do nothing about it.

Then there were only a few weeks left before my departure. Catching sight of myself in a mirror I was surprised at my appearance. I looked trim, brown, it seemed I was holding myself differently. I was really rather attractive, I thought, amused at my new-found vanity. When I went swimming I no longer minded if other people were there and sometimes even initiated conversations with them. I watched the women, saw their thighs gleaming under the water, noticing little rivulets of water running between their breasts. Their skin seemed to have so many colours trapped inside, like summer honey, I thought.

I wanted to see Carmen but a slight coolness had descended on our friendship, even though she had set up the meeting for me with the young writers. I would walk past her home and she would wave to me from her verandah, but she did not make a point of inviting me in.

I was out doing my grocery shopping when I saw a man in the plaza selling orchid plants. I bought one with a long spray of golden brown blooms and stopped at Carmen's house on my way home. To my utter discomfort, tears came to her eyes when I gave her the plant and she threw her arms around me in a warm hug. Her body felt wonderful, firm and full and I was sorry when she pulled away.

'Forgive me,' she said. 'I'm such a softie, now I've probably embarrassed you. It's so kind of you, I know just where I shall hang it.'

She hung it on a beam on the verandah and its long, golden bloom curved into the air between us. She busied herself making drinks and chatting about various things, the heat, Mr Anderson. A good man, she said, did his best to provide for his family and it couldn't be easy could it, not the way the economy was these days.

Carmen eventually stemmed the flow of chatter and we had a comfortable conversation. I promised to return the books she had lent me and remarked that, at first, I had found them difficult to read, but then I began to enjoy them.

'I've been stuck with Pope for too long,' I confessed. 'He was so safe.'

'Mind lightning don't strike you for such heresy,' she said and laughed, her bracelets tinkling along her arms.

That sound. It would be so difficult to leave.

It was very difficult to leave. Mr Anderson came round and seemed perplexed that I should be leaving. He was silent for a moment, looking around at the garden and then he looked at me with a little frown.

'But look at dat! I did tink you well an settle here and look how de garden look like someting at last. Even you yourself, you look different, look like you well an like it here.'

'Oh yes,' I laughed, 'I well an like it here.'

We sat in the kitchen and drank a Red Stripe together and I knew that I wanted very much to stay and felt tears coming into my eyes so that I had to get up and fuss with something in the refrigerator.

And Carmen. That last evening she helped me pack. She had bought me a lovely batik and I was touched that she would give me such a gift but she would not let me thank her, only got busy packing books into boxes. I was filled with a strange sort of languor and sat there quite useless but watching her hands at work filled me with panic.

'I can't believe I've accumulated so many things,' I said, to

143

break my own thoughts. 'Seems as if I have acquired more in the last few months than I have in the last several years.'

Carmen concentrated on taping up a box. 'Looks like you were settling in here,' she said.

'Yes and no,' I said. 'In some ways this has been the most unsettling few months of my life.' I looked at her, hoping she would understand. She looked at me and her face seemed to soften, her mouth parted as if she were about to say something, then she looked away and pulled out yet more books, yet another box and started packing them away carefully.

When we had finished packing she sat with me way into the night and my mind went round and round with a hundred crazy schemes for staying. But eventually she stood up, stretched her arms and said she must go. I walked her back to her house, holding her hand like an awkward teenager.

'I'll miss you my friend,' she said. She kissed me lightly on the cheek and hurried into her house.

As the plane lifted I craned to catch a last glimpse of the mountains. Some lines from the girl's novel came unexpectedly to me. Mama C had died and left the girl with a mass of old things to dispose of. She had put off dealing with the clutter but finally she resolved to sort it out. Most of it was horrible; old clothes, battered old shoes, dreadful things that the old woman had guarded, thinking people were just waiting for a chance to rob her of these, her valuable posessions. But the girl had come across an old china bowl that was used for serving rice and peas on Sundays, and a photograph of Mama C as a beautiful young woman and then she had wept, overcome with sadness for the old woman's bitter life, remembering that in her way, Mama C had loved her.

'I should have done this years ago,' she said. 'I have to learn what to keep and what to let go. And when I do throw it out, I have to learn not to lean back and use old sorrows to make new wounds.'

The mountains were out of sight but I seemed to see them vividly in my mind's eye. Early morning, late evening, their rich, complex colours, Carmen's face below the spray of golden orchids, the sound of her bracelets as she pushed open the gate. It all ran together in my mind, no, in my heart so that I felt a physical pain there and it spread throughout my body. I had wanted to hold her in my arms, but I did not know what to say. I had let myself grow old, dry out, immersed in other people's thoughts, writings, experiences. They were so much safer than accumulating my own, which might only turn out bitter, disappointing. But now, I was letting go of such thoughts, letting go of my own Mama C only, at such a very late stage. And now that I had found what I wanted to keep I did not know how to go about it. I turned my face towards the darkening window and wept.

Riding the Bus

At Cedar Rapids bus depot an elderly man in a red checkered shirt and blue suspenders, his hands folded against his belly, sleeps. His face is lined and creased like an old tortoise. A young boy with an up-tilted nose, a smooth cap of brown hair and aggressive acne scars smokes in short, sharp pulls. Country folk wait in the silent, clean building where ceiling fans whir us on to destinations with active names like Cedar Falls, Fort Dodge, Storm Lake and the sad Indian names they have chased away, Sioux City, Cherokee, Oskaloosa.

A man, in his thirties perhaps, starts talking to me. His hair is blond, fairly long to match his drooping moustache, his eyes a clear, Canada summer lake blue. He tells me about seeing cyclones in that part of the world. They are so strong they can make a straw stick into two by four. His daddy raises hogs but he hasn't seen him in eight years. He saw his mother last year. Not a family to keep in touch except at Christmas and Thanksgiving, he tells me. His brother raises hogs and he's on his way to see him. 'Just got out,' he says. 'From where?' 'Prison,' he says. 'Three years for D and D.' 'What's D and D?' 'Drunk driving,' he says. 'Did you,' I ask 'hit someone down?' 'No,' he says, the blue eyes clear, 'it was my fifth offence.' 'You going to stay off then?' I ask. 'Can if I want to,' he shrugs slightly. He has a little box, neatly taped, on the bench beside him, personal effects. He flicks a glance at a brown paper bag propped up beside the box. 'I been by the liquor store,' he laughs, a pleased, small noise. I nearly miss my bus for Storm Lake.

Seven hours on the bus through the flat Iowa landscape. I

146

read, I stare through the window. 'Welcome to Webster City –
Main Street USA. Population 8,900.' Cornfields, the movement
of the bus makes the furrows curve, their ends serrating the
horizon. A red barn, an oak tree, two phallic silos. So still and
empty everywhere. In a new country the trees keep their secrets.
They are strangers, that elm not grown against my leg, the
regular shape of that pine not printed in my palm and I have to
learn it all from the beginning. Into the empty landscape a clump
of brown birds flurries out of the brown grass, a monochrome
woodcut. No flowers, no clouds, even the river runs between
stern granite banks, Calvinist someone said later, hard man's
chest place refusing all adornment.

A late tractor driving into the sun raises a cloud of dust.
Sundown at the end of summer everything old gold and olive
green. The sun gave up and slipped away at Iowa Falls behind
St Matthews by the Bridge Episcopal Church. A hush, a moment
of drift before the evening star rises in splendid isolation.

The bus pulls up at a motel at Storm Lake. I climb out and
collect a key for a room. I open the door, switch on the light and
a ferocious blue velveteen bedspread growls at me. I back away
dropping my overnight bag and the virulent blue carpet snaps it
up. The walls are plastic, I walk to each in turn, not believing. I
need a drink but the nearest place is six blocks away and I know
that if I leave that room the bedspread will rise up to punish me
when I get back. Willie Lomas is in the room beside mine with a
woman whose skin looks like Brie cheese, white and weepy. Sorry
my friend, sorry for all the struggling musicians, salesmen,
writers who step into these plastic rooms with one fly buzzing
over the blue bedspread.

I sleep badly but in the morning the lake is not at all stormy
just flat and grey. The day is cold, bright and I spend it like a
silver dollar. I talk to students, reading poems to them of a hot
place, a luxurious, troubled female landscape with a rush of
colours, smells, flowers in trees, moss on the ground, vegetation
of all kinds coming round the corner to meet you. Their faces are
gentle. Most have grown up here, never been to New York which
they say is all muggings and danger. In this quiet, isolated place

I feel that my blood is running too fast, too red in my veins, my cells are replicating and dying off too quickly, my skin glows too bright. I try to hush myself, turn into a soft, brown teddy bear night time comfort. It doesn't work, I grow more brittle, strung out and all around me the gentle young faces smile and tell me about growing up, about brothers and sisters and I like them all and for a while I walk in and out of their homes, through their towns and feel incredibly grateful that our shared language makes it possible to travel with them for a while.

Back on the bus with a sea of old faces with yesterday's young faces tucked behind their eyes and the Greyhound is a warm old tabby cat carrying aunts and uncles to visit with little gifts in laminated shopping bags and there are two nuns who have brought their own sandwiches so that when we make a stop they don't have to rush in and wonder what to eat in the bright, busy bustle of the Diner. My companion is attractive, petite, a bright flirtatiousness in her mid-sixty year old face and I suddenly wish that she had some sexy man to make love to her in the nights after the bingo games and when she wins she buys bonds for her grandchildren and the eldest is homecoming queen this weekend and she will be there to see her all dressed up. She's wearing black, whoever heard of a homecoming queen in black, but she's a pretty little thing and no doubt she will look as nice as anything.

At a rest stop, my companion leaves the bus and a man leans over to talk to me through a haze of cigarette smoke.

'Where you from?'

'Jamaica.'

He looks at me suspiciously. 'I had a Jamaican friend once. Big, black guy he was. Can't remember his name now, we worked together. Construction site over near Mason City. I thought everybody in Jamaica was big and black.'

And male I think, but my travelling companion has returned to claim her seat and it would be too difficult to continue the conversation round her so I just smile at him but he looks unconvinced.

My companion is telling me that she's retired now. She was a nurse's aid, psychiatric ward mostly, terrible to see the young ones brought in, their brains fried like an egg on drugs and they'll never get better you know and I ask her who these kids are and she says all kinds I'm telling you, poor kids from the streets who don't know any better and rich college kids, all kinds I'm telling you and I tell her a story about my aunt who was also a psychiatric nurse, upstate New York hospital. One day, she was waiting for the bus, her car gone for servicing, she in her nurse's uniform out there in rural New York and this young man stops to give her a lift, well she hates to be late and there's no bus in sight so she sizes him up, looks decent enough, she takes a chance. They talk pleasantly on the way and she thanks him for the ride and later she tells a co-worker, now why's everyone so negative about the young people of today, why I met a young man, so nice, such good manners, so intelligent, really makes one optimistic about the future. Three days later they buzz her to come to admission, young man raving, bundle him into a strait-jacket, stab a sedative into him, trundle him off to a room and oh my God it's the very same young man. Brought in by the police, he was, seems he killed his mother, chopped her up into tiny pieces, wrapped them carefully and dropped them down the ventilator shafts of various subway stations.

'Well there you are,' my companion nods and we change the subject to talk of personal things. 'Did she think of marrying again?' She laughs, lights another cigarette and we're wrapped up in smoke at the back of the Greyhound tabby cat. 'No, at her age what would she get, some old man to get sick on her and she would have to take care of him and she's had quite enough of all that, thank you. She's retired now, does cleaning jobs, her time is her own, her money is her own and yes it would be nice to have a man, a healthy, vigorous man who is not going to start telling you to do this or do that and we are wrapped up there in a comfortable bond of agreement, happy to be healthy, vigorous women riding the Iowa bus.

A young woman in a severe grey suit with a spotless white blouse, boards the bus. Her name tag identifies her as Sister Rebecca. I wonder whose sister she is but I never find out. We

149

pull into the Iowa City bus stop and she is met by a group of spotlessly clean young men but they are not her brothers, they are Elders. I suddenly remember a young Nigerian writer who earnestly inquired which direction was East. Our exiled Iranian poet widened his expressive brown eyes but said nothing. In her country, she tells us, she cannot attend the mosque but she is nevertheless assiduous in her devotions. My taxi driver reverses into the Mormons' luggage, apologises to them without warmth and puts the cab into forward gear. I wonder what he is thinking.

Through the window I see my friend from the bus being met by a harried woman with assorted children piled into a station wagon. I wave at her and she gives me a little wave and a brief conspiratorial wink.

Winter is coming and the streets have a cold, empty look. A trickle of rain washes away the lingering warmth of the bus but I am buoyed up by that sparkling little wink. Hope it won't rain for the homecoming queen.